TRUCKIN' INTO TROUBLE

Frank's right hand was anchored to the door handle of the eighteen-wheeler by the handcuffs, but he reached his left hand back, extending himself as far as possible. He missed the crank that connected the rig to the cab by a couple of feet. It was obvious that he couldn't possibly reach the handle that way.

The truck hurtled around a sharp turn, and Frank's door flew wide open. For a moment he dangled just above the onrushing asphalt road. Grabbing frantically for the door frame with his left hand, he pulled himself back against the side of the cab.

"I'll never get it this way," he gasped.

"Hurry, Frank!" Pat screamed. "I can't keep us on the road much longer!"

Books in THE HARDY BOYS CASEFILES® Series

Available from ARCHWAY Paperbacks

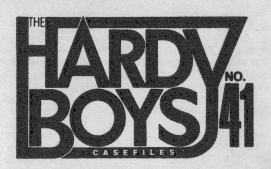

THE HARDY BOYS NO. 41
CASEFILES

HIGHWAY ROBBERY

FRANKLIN W. DIXON

AN ARCHWAY PAPERBACK
Published by POCKET BOOKS
New York   London   Toronto   Sydney   Tokyo   Singapore

Ingram 7/2/90 #2.95

AN ARCHWAY PAPERBACK *Original*

An Archway Paperback published by
POCKET BOOKS, a division of Simon & Schuster Inc.
1230 Avenue of the Americas, New York, NY 10020

Copyright © 1990 by Simon & Schuster Inc.
Cover art copyright © 1990 Brian Kotzky
Produced by Mega-Books of New York, Inc.

ISBN: 0-671-70038-3

First Archway Paperback printing July 1990

10 9 8 7 6 5 4 3 2 1

THE HARDY BOYS, AN ARCHWAY PAPERBACK
and colophon are registered trademarks of Simon & Schuster Inc.

THE HARDY BOYS CASEFILES is a trademark
of Simon & Schuster Inc.

Printed in the U.S.A.

IL 7+

Chapter

1

"HOW CAN YOU listen to that noise?" asked the blond young man. He snatched up a compact disk and held it out in front of him as if it were contaminated. "It's got no beat, it's got no soul." He regarded his companion with disbelief and disgust. "You've got no taste!"

"Oh, right! *You're* going to talk to *me* about good taste. Wonderful!" The tall guy who was now speaking had brown hair and a lean build. "You know, I think your ears have been blown out from all the junk you listen to."

The argument was taking place next to a rack of CDs in a music store at the Bayport Mall. The blond guy stood six feet tall, while the darker one was an inch taller. Both appeared to be in excellent shape. If it came to a fight, they would be evenly matched.

Between them was another young man, about five inches shorter and twenty pounds lighter than the two who were arguing. Glancing from one to the other, the small guy had his hands up, ready to separate them by force if he had to.

"Hey, whoa! Take it easy, you two. Remember brotherly love, and all that good stuff? Don't forget—I work next door. You two are going to scare away all our customers. So if you start getting rough, I'll just have to deck both of you."

The two Hardy brothers looked at him, then at each other, and burst into laughter.

"We're cool, Tony," said Joe Hardy, the blond, shaking his head. "I'm just trying to make him see the light. He doesn't know good music from garbage."

Joe's brother, Frank, eighteen and a year older than his brother, gave Tony a look of mock sorrow. "He's the one who's a hopeless case. He embarrasses the whole family. Joe wouldn't know good music if it bit him in the leg. But the thing that *really* gets me is that he insists on putting that noise on our CD player, and I have to hear it. Talk about pollution!"

"At least you two *have* a CD player," said Tony with a sigh.

Tony Prito was a longtime friend of the Hardy brothers. Though not big, he was wiry, with lightning reflexes. He was a standout second baseman on their high school baseball team and a dangerous pass receiver in football. "I figure it'll be another month's work at Mr. Pizza before I can afford one, even with a special break on the price."

"How do you rate a special break?" asked Joe. "You have friends in high places?"

"Not *high* places, just the *right* places," Tony said, grinning back. "My uncle, Matt Simone, has a long-haul trucking company. One of his clients is Ultratech Electronics, and my cousin Mike, who drives for them, says he can get me an Ultratech at cost. You can't beat that, right?"

"Ultratech?" asked a new voice. The three boys turned to see Jeff Lanier, someone they knew slightly from Bayport High. Jeff's pale face was framed by black hair that he kept perfectly in place. He was very particular about his clothes and paid careful attention to what was in. He didn't have time for after-school activities because he spent all his spare time at the mall. He considered himself a big deal with the girls, although most girls wouldn't agree with him.

"I don't have a cousin to help *me* out, but I bet you won't beat the deal *I* got on an Ultratech CD player last week."

"How much?" asked Frank. He didn't like Jeff and hoped that it didn't show. A second later he decided Jeff wouldn't notice. It would never occur to him that anyone could dislike him.

3

With a self-satisfied smirk, Jeff told them what he'd paid. Tony let out a low whistle.

"Hey, that *is* a deal! At that price, I could buy one today! Where'd you pick it up?" he asked eagerly.

"At a place out on Route Nineteen," replied Jeff. "It doesn't look like much. Just a kind of grungy warehouse with a lot of stuff on the floor in boxes—CD players, tape decks, everything. But the prices are, like, *unreal*."

Joe and Frank exchanged a quick look. "So how'd you find this place?" asked Joe. As far as he was concerned, it *did* sound "unreal"—and probably more than a little shady. "Was there an ad in the paper, or what?"

"Ad in the paper!" echoed Jeff scornfully. "No way, Jose! That's how they keep their prices down. No advertising. And no fancy signs or decorations, either. I just heard about it from some dude, I can't remember who exactly."

"Where is it? How do I get there?" Tony cut in. He gazed expectantly at the Hardys. "Maybe we can take a drive out there sometime."

Jeff's directions were complicated so Frank jotted them down. The warehouse was outside Bayport in an area they didn't know very well.

"Hey, thanks!" called Tony as Jeff headed for the exit.

"No sweat," Jeff answered, not looking back.

" 'No way, Jose,' " mimicked Frank. "Now, there's a guy who'll never be lonely as long as he has a mirror."

"Right," agreed Joe. "The guy never wears the same clothes twice. He must have a three-acre closet. I heard he keeps a blow-dryer in his locker at school."

Tony was impatient, hopping from foot to foot. "What do you say? I don't work any more today. Let's head on over to this place, okay? Maybe there's something there you'd be interested in, too."

"Tony," Joe said quietly. "You said that your cousin could get you an Ultratech at cost, right?"

"Right."

"And Jeff said he paid a lot *less* than that, right?"

"Yeah," said Tony slowly. He was now frowning suspiciously. "What's your point?"

Frank took a quick look around. A number of other shoppers were within earshot. "Why don't we take this conversation someplace else?" he suggested.

The three young men walked out of the store into the busy traffic of the mall's arcade.

As they walked, Frank spoke. "One thing we've learned from our dad, Tony. Things that sound too good to be true usually are."

Fenton Hardy, Frank and Joe's father, had spent a number of years as a New York City detective before beginning practice as a private investigator. Now he was an internationally known detective.

A light dawned in Tony's eyes. "You think maybe . . ."

"Tony," Joe cut in, "think about it. When stuff like this is being sold for less than what the manufacturer gets for it, out of a grungy warehouse that doesn't advertise except by word of mouth, you have to figure that the stuff is probably hot."

Tony stared at Joe and then scowled. "Well—hey, maybe there's some other reason! Maybe these are models they've stopped making now and need to get rid of. Or they got some kind of special discount from the factory because—oh, I don't know! All I know is, I want to check it out. You have a problem with that?"

Frank shrugged. "I guess not." He turned to Joe. "You know, I *am* kind of curious about this setup. It might be interesting to see—*especially* if it is some kind of fencing operation. Why don't we take a ride out there and look around?"

Joe held up a hand in warning. "The whole operation sounds like it's probably illegal."

"Don't worry, Joe, if it's crooked, I'm gone. No way am I buying stolen goods," Tony said.

"The place will probably be closed by the time we get there," Joe said. "But, who cares, I've got nothing better to do. Let's hit the road. The van's out in G parking lot."

Joe got behind the wheel of the black customized van he and Frank owned. Frank sat beside him with Jeff's directions, and Tony rode in the backseat. It was late afternoon on a perfect summer day, and they rode with the windows open.

The area they were driving through had clearly seen better days. Aside from a few gas stations and convenience stores, Joe noticed that most of the buildings were industrial and many were empty. Everything looked run-down.

"Talk about your basic low-rent district," he muttered as they turned onto Route 19. "This has got to be the lowest."

Frank nodded. "It may not be the end of the world, but I bet you can see it from here."

"That's how they keep the prices down," said Tony. But Joe didn't think Tony sounded so convinced anymore. It wasn't a likely setting for an honest retail business.

They'd been on the road almost an hour, when Frank looked up from the directions. "It should be up ahead, on the left. There it is!"

There was no sign identifying the place, but some numbers were hand-painted on a piece of wood that hung from a chain-link fence. The address matched the one in Jeff's directions.

Joe steered the van through an opening in the fence and into a parking area. Only two other cars were there, and beyond them stood a shabby one-story building.

"Business isn't exactly booming," Joe noted dryly as he parked the van.

"So, what does that prove?" demanded Tony.

"Nothing, that's what! Let's go in and see what's happening."

"It looks closed," Frank said.

Tony walked ahead impatiently. "There are lights on." He tried the door, and when it swung inward, he entered, followed by Frank and Joe.

By the pale light of two strips of hanging fluorescent tubes, Frank saw a large, mostly empty space with no windows. A door, possibly leading to an office, was off to one side. Other than a few cartons on the floor, there was nothing to be seen. No people. No stereo components. Nothing.

For a second the boys stood and stared silently. Then Tony said, "Could be it's the wrong place."

They paused at the sound of a noise from behind the office door. Frank pointed. "Maybe whoever's in there can tell us something."

They started toward the door, but before they reached it, the door opened and two men appeared.

"Excuse us—" Tony began, and then stopped short.

The two strangers froze at the sight of the three boys. In their jumpsuits, gloves, and heavy shoes, the men looked like warehouse workers, except for one detail—their startled eyes peering out from behind wool ski masks!

Chapter

2

THE TWO INTRUDERS recovered and made a quick dash for the front door. The smaller of the two rammed a shoulder into Tony's ribs and knocked him flat.

The second man, who was as tall as the Hardys and more solidly built, carried a briefcase in one hand. He showed amazing quickness for his size and surprised the brothers by dodging between them instead of making an end run around them. Joe dived for the legs of the running man, but all he caught was the heel of a heavy shoe in his forehead. Dazed from the impact, he lay sprawled on the floor.

Coming to a stop, Frank checked on his brother and Tony. The men in masks were out the door and into their car.

"Joe?" asked Frank. He heard a car engine roar to life outside and tires squeal as the car sped away. "Hey, Joe! You hear me?" Nearby, Tony was slowly pushing himself up onto his hands and knees, wheezing painfully as he struggled for breath.

"I'm all right," Joe said weakly. "I'm okay. Where did they—did those guys get away?"

"They're gone," Frank replied, helping Joe stand up. "They should've known that the *last* way to hurt you is to kick you in the head. Tony?" Frank looked over at his friend, who was still on his knees, feeling his ribs and wincing. "You need a hand? How are you doing?"

"Whoof," gasped Tony. "I feel like I just got trampled by the Chicago Bears. *All* of them. But I don't think anything's broken, just bruised a little."

Once all three were standing again, Joe suggested, "We'd better see what they left behind. They were doing something in that room."

"And you don't need ski masks to do bookkeeping or sweep the floors," added Frank. He pulled out a handkerchief and wrapped his hand in it. "It'd be better not to leave a lot of fingerprints around. We don't want to mess things up if the police get called in here," he explained to Tony.

Tony nodded slowly, his eyes widening. "Oh, yeah, good idea. What do you think they—"

"No point in guessing," Frank said. He gently

pushed against the door to open it fully, but it wouldn't move any more. Something was lying behind it. The room was unlit, except for what little light spilled in from the warehouse. Frank walked into the room and then stiffened, drawing his breath in sharply. He looked out through the doorway and called to his brother. "Joe, get the flashlight from the van, quick! There's a body in here!"

Joe raced outside. He returned quickly, carrying a powerful flashlight. Switching it on, he pointed its bright beam into the small dark room. Joe knew at once that the man lying sprawled on the floor was dead.

He played the light over the rest of the room and saw a metal filing cabinet with its drawers pulled out, apparently empty. A telephone lay by the dead man, its wires slashed.

"They may have cleaned out some papers," said Joe. "We'd better call the police."

"We're outside the city limits," Frank pointed out. "This is County Sheriff territory, not Bayport PD. We'd better find a phone." He noticed Tony's quizzical expression. "The phone in the van is broken."

"We passed a convenience store not too far from here," Tony said, his voice shaky. "There was a booth outside."

"I'll go," Joe said.

"I'll come too," said Tony, backing away from the office. "If—if it's okay with you, Frank."

11

"Go ahead, it's cool."

As he started out with Joe, Tony noticed an empty carton on the floor.

"It's for an Ultratech cassette deck," he said, pointing to it. "This was the right place after all."

"But the sale is over," replied Frank.

Joe and Tony returned just a couple of minutes before the first carload of sheriff's deputies rolled in. Frank and Joe had a few contacts and even a couple of friends among the Bayport police, but they didn't know anyone in the county force.

An officer took their statements, and then told the boys to wait while he talked to his superior officer.

The man in charge appeared to be in his late forties. He was tall and lanky, with a deeply tanned face and gray-tinted eyeglasses in silver frames. As he listened to the junior officer's report, he nodded and glanced over at the Hardys and Tony a couple of times. After the younger man had finished, he silently studied the three for a minute before walking over to them. He held their statements in one hand.

"I'm Chief Deputy MacReedy," he said. "Which one of you is Tony Prito?"

"I am." Tony stepped forward.

MacReedy looked Tony up and down, saying nothing. Finally he studied the notes in his hand.

"Frank and Joe Hardy, huh? Would you happen to be Fenton Hardy's kids?"

"Yes, sir," answered Frank. "Do you know him?"

"We've met," said the deputy. There was another silence, which was broken by Joe.

"Do you know who the dead guy is?"

MacReedy's head shot up, and he fixed Joe with a steely look from behind his glasses. He walked over to Joe and stopped when their faces were inches apart.

"Now, listen. We'd better get something straight here and now, son, or you and I won't get along at all. *I'm* the one who asks the questions, and *you're* the one who answers them. And those answers better be good. That clear?"

Joe's eyes flashed for a moment, but all he said was, "yes."

"That pretty van outside belong to you?"

"Yes, sir," said Frank. He gave Joe a look that conveyed the message *stay cool*. They knew the deputy was being a major jerk, but it wouldn't do to get on his bad side.

"Very nice. A real fancy set of wheels. Your daddy must be doing real well at the detective business to buy his boys a nice toy like that."

"He didn't—" Joe started to say, and the deputy cut him off with an upraised palm.

MacReedy began to pace back and forth in front of the three boys, speaking as he moved. "Now, I ask myself what three fellows like you in that customized, souped-up machine are doing out here, on the wrong side of the tracks.''

"It was my idea," Tony said. "Like I told the other officer—"

"That's 'deputy,' son."

"Yes, sir," Tony said nervously. "Like I told him, I heard that there was a place around here where you could get stereo equipment at a really great price."

"Yeah, I know what you *said*," snapped MacReedy. "But I bet you can come up with a better story if you try real hard. One I might actually believe."

"We're telling you the truth," Frank insisted.

"That so?" MacReedy abruptly stopped his pacing and turned to face them. "I have a buddy who's a Bayport cop. I've heard all about you two—how you always turn up at crime scenes— *before* the police as often as not. How you get underfoot and try to do their jobs for them.

"Well, I don't want you thinking you can get away with playing junior cop on a case of mine. Just because I've got no cause to bring you in right now doesn't mean I buy that line about shopping for stereos. I've got my eye on you."

Joe said, "Wait a—"

"Don't you dare interrupt me!" MacReedy's voice cut like a whip. He reached out a long arm and pointed a finger at Joe, Frank, and Tony in turn.

"Now listen up, and keep those lips buttoned.

If I hear that you've been snooping around, asking questions, sticking your noses in where they don't belong, I'm going to land on you with both feet. There won't be a thing your daddy will be able to do for you then. Now you three get in that van and get out of here. And stay out of my way! If I want you I'll send for you."

With that, the deputy wheeled around and stalked away. Frank watched a muscle twitch in Joe's jaw, and he reached out to steady him.

"Let's get moving," he urged. "There's nothing we can do here except buy into some major trouble."

Joe took a deep breath and slowly relaxed. But after they went outside and climbed back into the van, he whispered to Frank, "Wouldn't you love to solve this thing and rub his face in it?"

Soon after they pulled out of the parking lot, Tony leaned forward and asked, "Joe, would you stop at that phone booth again? I want to call home and let them know where I am."

They stopped a minute later, and Tony went to use the phone. "Did you get the idea that there's some kind of history between Dad and this MacReedy?" asked Frank.

"Loud and clear," Joe said. "I don't think they were good buddies, either. Let's ask Dad about him when we get home. Here's Tony."

Tony slowly climbed into the backseat. His face had gone pale, and he looked even worse than he had after they'd found the body.

"Tony?" Frank asked. "What's the matter? You look real shook up."

Tony didn't say anything for a moment. Then he said softly, "It's—my cousin Mike."

"What's the problem?" asked Joe, worried.

"He was driving a truckload of Ultratech components and a bunch of goons forced him to stop. When Mike realized that they were going to hijack his goods, he tried to fight them off. They beat him up—bad. He's in the hospital."

Chapter

3

"I WANT TO GET over there right away," Tony said anxiously.

"Sure." Joe started up the van. "We'll take you there right now."

Forty-five minutes later they arrived at the hospital and were directed to a room on the seventh floor.

Tony's cousin Mike Simone was a muscular man in his thirties, but lying in the hospital bed he appeared to be fragile. Some curls of black hair stuck out from the bandages wrapped around his head. His left arm was in a cast, and his face was swollen and bruised. In addition to his visible injuries, Mike had a cracked rib.

The boys noticed, though, that the look in Mike's eyes wasn't so much one of pain as it was of anger.

"If it had been two guys, I would've taken them," Mike muttered. "But four was too many."

"How long will you be laid up?" Tony asked. He sat in a chair beside his cousin, while Joe and Frank leaned against a window sill.

"I may be out of here as early as the day after tomorrow once they're sure my head's okay." Mike sagged back against the pillows and closed his eyes. "But I don't know when I'll be able to drive a rig again. This arm won't be much good for maybe two months."

"How'd it happen, anyway?" Joe asked. "If you don't mind talking about it."

"No, I don't mind," said Mike. "I had just left Bayport, heading north. There's a shortcut I always use between two interstates, kind of a deserted stretch of road. About halfway along this, I see these traffic barriers and flashing lights. A guy was standing there in one of those orange vests, waving a red flag.

"I figure there's some kind of accident up ahead, so I pull over. Three guys in ski masks with blackjacks or clubs or something jump up on the cab and yank both doors open. Then the guy in the vest drops his flag and pulls a mask down over *his* face."

At the mention of ski masks, Frank and Joe exchanged a look. Mike went on.

"I had a baseball bat under the seat, and I grabbed it and tried to belt one of them, but they pulled me down from the cab and—the last thing

I remember was getting something real hard bounced off my skull. A woman driving a car found me lying on the road a little while later. The truck was gone."

"You could have been killed, Mike!" Tony stood up and stared down at his cousin. "Why go up against four guys like that? For what? A bunch of electronics?"

Mike nodded and sighed. "I won't argue, kid. I was stupid. But—see, there's things going on here that you don't understand."

"Like what?"

Mike was silent. He glanced at Frank and Joe. Quickly Frank suggested, "Tony, why don't we wait outside for you?"

"No, wait, Frank," Tony said. "Mike, these are my buddies, and I trust them. I guarantee anything you say will be kept confidential."

Mike thought a moment and then said, "Okay, Tony, if you say so. Pop probably won't like me talking, but—this is just between us, right?"

"You got it," Joe said.

"All right. My dad owns this shipping outfit, Lombard Hauling. We're just a family company with a small list of clients we transport goods for. Our biggest client is Ultratech Electronics."

"And their shipment got taken today," said Frank.

"The thing is," said Mike, "this isn't the first Ultratech shipment to be hijacked. It's the third."

"The third!" echoed Tony with disbelief. "How come you haven't said anything—"

Mike held up his good hand. "Tony, if it was up to me, this wouldn't be news to you now. But Pop has played it real close for some reason. The company is really hurting, Tony. I'm scared that we could lose Ultratech as a client, and our insurance, too. And then Lombard Hauling would be out of business."

"What did the police say?" asked Frank.

Tony bit his lip. "We reported the first hijacking so we could get the insurance money for Ultratech. But Pop wouldn't go to the sheriff last time, and he won't go this time, either. When he was here earlier we had a big argument about it. He just won't go, and he won't say why, either. I tried to convince him, but—"

"That's crazy!" Tony burst out. "Uncle Matt can't—"

"Hold it, Tony," said Frank. "Mike, how do you think your father would feel about bringing in private investigators?"

"The kind of people who know how to find things out, *and* keep their mouths shut," added Joe.

"I don't know," Mike said, shaking his head. "Why? You have some in mind?"

"We do, actually," Frank said. "Our father, Fenton Hardy, is one of the best private operatives there is—"

"The thing is," said Mike, "we're sort of strapped for cash right now."

"Well, we have a kind of family business, too, and my dad wouldn't press you," Joe said. "Frank and I are sort of junior partners."

"Hold on a minute," Mike interrupted. "I don't want to sound ungrateful, but this hijacking business is no game." He pointed to his bandaged head. "They play rough."

"No, really, Mike," said Tony. "Frank and Joe are for real. They've gotten into some heavy scenes, and they can take care of themselves."

"We're good at finding things out," Frank added with a smile.

Mike stared at the Hardys. "You're serious, aren't you?"

"Could you figure out some way of setting us up with jobs at Lombard, as a cover?" Frank asked. "At least we could look around."

"It couldn't do any harm," added Joe.

Mike nodded. "Let me call Pop," he said. "He had to go back to the office. He's probably still there."

The phone conversation was short, and Mike didn't do much of the talking. When he hung up, he seemed to be shaken and disturbed.

"What's up?" Tony asked.

"Ultratech gave Pop a rough time," Mike replied. "They said they're thinking of finding another trucking company, one that does a better job of keeping its shipments safe. And then, he said, the law just paid him a little visit.''

"I thought you said the sheriff's office didn't know about the hijacking,'' Joe said.

"No, this was about something else. They found a body around five o'clock today, a guy who'd been murdered, somewhere near Bayport.''

Tony was about to tell Mike about their experience at the warehouse, but he caught a warning look from Frank and kept quiet.

"What does the body have to do with Lombard Hauling?'' Joe asked.

"The cops said the guy was a small-time gangster named Mickey Vane. He had a fairly long record. Well, he once worked for Lombard as a driver. Pop told the deputy that he didn't know anything about his record, but the deputy didn't seem to believe him. And Pop says the deputy's on his way over here to question me.'' Mike let out a sigh, then added, "Oh, he did say he'd talk to Frank and Joe about this investigation tomorrow morning at the office.''

"What can *you* tell the law?'' asked Tony.

"Me? Nothing,'' Mike said. "But it sounds like this cop who questioned Pop is a rough customer. He all but said that he suspected Pop of being mixed up with this Vane guy in some kind of dirty business. Pop almost threw him out of the office.''

"Mike,'' said Frank. "You said that these hijackers stopped you on a pretty deserted road that you used as a shortcut, right?''

"Right. Driving a rig, you're always trying to save a little time and gas.''

"The thing is," Frank went on, "if this was a shortcut, how many people could have known you'd be there?''

Mike gave Frank a troubled look. "You mean, is there somebody inside the company that's part of this gang? Yeah, I've thought the same thing. Maybe that's why Pop didn't want the police involved. Maybe he's scared that there's a crook at Lombard, and that it might even be one of the family.''

"Impossible," said Tony flatly.

"Well, even the other employees are *like* family to Pop. If someone there is bent, he'd handle it quietly, without—''

There was a knock at the door, and a nurse entered, looking flustered.

"Mr. Simone, there's a-an officer here who insists on talking to you right now. I told him that you were resting, but he said—''

A brusque voice interrupted the nurse. "I said I didn't have time to waste. He'll talk to me, and talk right *now*.''

A tall man in a khaki uniform brushed past the outraged nurse, and for the second time that day Tony and the Hardys found themselves looking into the hard eyes of Chief Deputy MacReedy.

Joe felt anger rise in him as he watched the officer's eyes narrow.

"You three again," MacReedy said, his lips compressing into a thin line. "The way I keep tripping over you, you boys are bound to end up in a jail cell!"

Chapter

4

"ALL RIGHT," said MacReedy, "let's hear your story *this* time. What are you boys shopping for at the hospital?"

"Just paying a get-well call on Tony's cousin," Frank said quickly.

"That's right, Chief Deputy," Joe added. "We're cheering him up with our presence."

"Well, boys, your presence doesn't work that way on me," MacReedy answered curtly. "I've had my fill of you. Visiting hours are over, so you three beat it while Mr. Simone and I talk."

"I have nothing to tell you," Mike said.

"Oh, you'd be surprised what you know," purred MacReedy. He glanced back at Frank and Joe and Tony. "You still here? I told you to move. Now do it."

"Take it easy, Mike," said Tony. He filed out of the room behind the Hardys.

Back in the van, Tony asked, "Why didn't you want me to tell Mike about finding that body?"

"Just being careful," said Frank.

Tony sounded insulted. "Hey, you think my cousin Mike is a crook?"

"Take it easy, Tony. We don't think anything like that," Joe assured him. "When we're working on a case, we like to keep information on a need-to-know basis. We trust Mike, but we don't know who he might talk to, or who *they* might talk to. See what I mean?"

"It's habit," Frank went on. "It keeps our cases more contained. Less chance for leaks."

"Well, all right, if you say so," Tony agreed.

Frank and Joe dropped Tony off at his house. Before driving away, they arranged to pick him up the next morning so he could introduce them to his uncle Matt.

Back at their house Frank and Joe found their father in his office, and they started to fill him in on their day. When they mentioned Chief Deputy MacReedy, Fenton narrowed his eyes.

"MacReedy?" he asked. "Kind of a rangy fellow with a bad temper?"

"That sounds like him," said Joe. "You two ever have a run-in of any kind?"

Fenton nodded. "When I first started in business here, I was hired to work on a fraud case.

MacReedy was investigating it for the sheriff's office. He seemed like a good man, but a little too—in those days we called him too gung-ho. You felt he might get carried away in a situation, forget about procedure, cut a corner—that kind of thing.

"Well, he made an arrest," Fenton went on, "but he tampered with some evidence in order to nail it down tight, so he lost the perpetrator and went up on charges. Somehow he got it into his head that I was responsible, and ever since he's held it against me."

"That's a long time to hold a grudge," Frank commented.

Fenton leaned forward. "You don't want to get on his bad side. But since he knows you're my sons, you're already there. Steer clear of him as much as possible, boys."

"We'll try," Joe told their father. "But it looks like what he's working on connects with our investigation."

"Are you sure?" asked Fenton.

Frank nodded. "First, the dead man once worked for Lombard Hauling. Second, the hot goods that were being sold at that warehouse were made by Ultratech, and that's what has been hijacked." As he spoke he counted off the points on his fingers.

"By the way, Dad, could you look into a couple of things for us?" Joe asked.

"If I can. What do you need?"

"We need to know the record of this Mickey Vane—he's the one who got killed today."

"It'd be good to find out who owns the warehouse where they were selling the stolen electronics, too," said Frank. "And who was renting it and for how long."

They gave Fenton the address. As they were about to leave his office, he called out, "Frank? Joe? I know that you know how to watch out for yourselves, but you should really stay away from Lamar MacReedy." Fenton sounded casual, but Frank and Joe knew that he was concerned. "He'd be happy to have any excuse to get at you, if only to get back at me."

"We'll keep our heads down, Dad," replied Joe.

The next morning Frank, Joe, and Tony drove over to Lombard Hauling. Joe pulled the van in through the open gate and parked next to a medium-size garage with a loading dock on one side. A few small buildings were attached to the rear of the garage. Probably offices, Joe decided. Near the loading dock he saw a couple of mechanics working on tall, boxy truck cabs. A few trailers with *Lombard* painted on the sides in red stood empty, ready to receive the next loads. The place smelled familiar to Joe—gasoline, oil, and grease—all blended.

Tony led them past the garage to an outdoor entrance to the first building. Just as he raised his hand to knock, an angry voice pierced through the closed door and stopped him.

"You'll be hearing from us again, and you won't like it!" The door swung open and a middle-aged man in a lime green sports jacket and open-necked shirt stalked out. He was balding and stocky, with a pug nose and an angry flush on his face. He shoved between Frank and Joe and marched off.

"Uncle Matt?" called Tony.

"Come on in." Frank and Joe followed Tony inside to an office, where a tall, powerful-looking man was standing behind a desk. His sleeves were rolled up above his elbows, showing muscular arms. He looked like an older version of Mike, with close-trimmed frizzy white hair.

Frank checked out the office curiously. It wasn't exactly a plush office. The scarred wooden desk was stacked high with papers and folders that almost hid the phone. Maps tacked to the walls had routes drawn across them in felt-tip pen. The only other wall decoration was a calendar with a color photograph of a flashy customized truck.

"Who was *that?*" Tony asked his uncle.

"Aah." Matt waved a hand in disgust. "Lou Gerard. The union's new business agent for the local our people belong to. Forget about him."

He looked curiously at the Hardys.

Tony quickly jumped in. "Uncle Matt, this is

Frank and Joe Hardy, the ones Mike told you about last night.''

Matt sat back in his desk chair, his eyes still on Frank and Joe. "When Mike said something about detectives, he didn't mention you were *kids*. I don't know—"

"Uncle Matt," Tony said, "trust me. These two really get around. They may be young, but they aren't helpless. Go ahead, give them a try."

Matt shrugged. "How old are you two?"

"I'm eighteen," Frank answered, "and Joe is seventeen."

"Okay. Joe, legally you have to be eighteen to even start learning big rigs. I guess we can say you're an apprentice mechanic. Frank, you're too young to actually drive a rig, but you can be a driver's helper. You'll work with Pat Mulvaney, our top driver, until Mike gets back."

There was a knock at Matt's door, and a second later a man came in with a sheaf of papers. He had sandy hair and freckles, and several pens stuck out of a plastic pocket protector in his shirt.

"Frank, Joe, this is Felix Kinney," said Matt. "Frank and Joe are starting to work here, Felix. Felix is our numbers man—in charge of billing, schedules, bookkeeping."

Felix smiled and then said softly, "What there is of it these days, what with—"

"All right, Felix," Matt cut in gruffly. "Leave the papers and get back to work. And ask Pat to come in here."

After Felix had gone, Matt tilted his chair back against the wall behind him. "All right. What can I tell you?"

"Just fill us in on what's been going down," said Joe.

Matt nodded. "There have been three hijackings, all of Ultratech equipment. Every time the truck was completely cleaned out. On the first heist, I brought in the sheriff and my insurance paid Ultratech for the loss. The second time I was worried about how my insurance people would react, so I kept quiet and paid for the loss myself."

"What about this one?" Frank asked.

Matt sighed and shook his head. "I'll be able to cover this one, too—barely. But if there's another one—I don't know. It would just finish us. Some of my men are already talking about finding new jobs, before these are shot out from under them."

"This man Mickey Vane—" Frank began.

Matt glared up at him. "How do you know about him?" he demanded.

"We were at the hospital with Mike last night, when that deputy arrived," said Joe.

"Well, I can't tell you much," Matt said. "I hired him two years back, before I found out he had a record. If he'd told me about it up front, I might have kept him, but since he lied, I let him go as soon as I found out. I hadn't heard of him again till last night."

"Did MacReedy tell you that stolen Ultratech products were being sold out of the place where Vane's body was found?" Joe asked.

Matt's eyes widened. "No, he didn't. Unless— maybe he suspects *I* had something to do with it, but that's crazy!" His jaw clenched.

"Let that go for now," said Frank. "What's the problem between you and this man Lou Gerard?"

Matt's face took on a stony look. "Nothing. Forget about him. That's private business."

Frank shot Matt a probing look. "We can do our job only if you level with us."

Matt said nothing.

After an awkward silence, Tony said, "Well, I've got to get to work. I'll catch a bus outside. See you, guys, Uncle Matt."

"Tony!" Matt called out. "I'm trusting you not to tell your mother and father about any of this. There's no point in worrying them. Right?"

"If you say so, Uncle Matt," answered Tony, but he seemed a little uncomfortable with the idea.

Just after Tony left, a woman entered Matt's office. In her midforties, she was tall and fair with light brown hair. Her jeans and work shirt were grease stained.

Matt smiled. "Pat! Come in, sit down. This is Joe Hardy. He'll be learning the ropes in the garage. And his brother, Frank, here, is going to crew with you as your helper. Boys, meet Pat Mulvaney."

As they exchanged hellos, Pat noticed Joe staring at her. "Something wrong, Joe?"

Joe's face got red. "Well, no—I figured—that is, you're a *woman!*".

Matt laughed. "Say, you *are* a detective, aren't you! She's a fine driver, too. And she happens to be my wife's sister. She's someone I need and trust. So I want to let her in on why you two are here."

Pat listened, looking Frank over carefully as Matt explained. "You look healthy enough," she said with a smile. "It's about time Matt got someone to help get those crooks." Pat turned and headed back out the office door. "When you're finished talking with Matt, come out to the garage and I'll start your lessons."

After she'd gone, Joe said, "Mr. Simone—"

"Please. Make it 'Matt.' "

"Okay, Matt. I'm sure you're right to trust Pat about who we are, but—"

"Pat's my right arm around here," Matt interrupted, frowning.

Frank could see how defensive and gruff Matt was, but they had to get him to understand how important it was to maintain secrecy. Leaning forward, he tried to pick up where Joe had left off. "Matt, what you have to understand—"

Frank stopped abruptly as a shrill scream from the garage echoed through the room!

Chapter

5

MATT JUMPED UP and ran out of the office into the garage, Frank and Joe at his heels. The workers inside were staring at Pat Mulvaney, who was comforting a pretty dark-haired girl. The girl was shaking and trying to hold back tears.

"I-I'm s-s-sorry, I—it was just that I didn't expect it. . . ." the girl stammered.

"What happened?" Matt demanded when he reached them.

Pat's face was grim. "Teri wanted some papers that I'd put in the cab of this truck. She opened it—and found this."

Pat reached up into the cab and pulled out a large rat with a paper tied around its neck. "Is this someone's idea of a joke?" she asked no one in particular.

Joe took the rat from her and handed it to Matt.

"Is it—is that—real?" Teri asked with a small shiver. "Is it—dead?"

"It's not real," Joe reassured her. Just then he took a good look and noticed how cute Teri was, even though she was still terrified. "It's just an imitation, the kind of thing you'd buy in a joke shop. But it does look gross, all right."

Matt opened the note and studied it. Frank and Joe leaned in to read what had been printed in large block letters. It said: "RATS GET HURT WHEN THEY WON'T WISE UP."

Matt crumpled the note in his fist, his face red with anger. "When was this put here? You have any idea?"

"It could've happened any time since I pulled in yesterday," said Pat. "There've been a lot of people around."

Matt turned to the girl. "Teri, are you all right? It was just someone's bad idea of a joke, that's all."

Teri smiled weakly. "I know, it just caught me by surprise. What does that note mean? It sounds like a threat. Is someone mad at Pat?"

Matt shook his head. "No, honey, it's supposed to be a joke, and the joke is supposed to be on me." Joe was hoping Matt would explain what the so-called joke was about, but he obviously didn't want to talk about it. Matt just smiled at Teri and changed the subject. "Oh, hey, let me make some introductions, here. Frank, Joe, this is Teri Yarnell. She works with Felix on the books. Frank and Joe Hardy are our newest employees, Teri. Joe and Teri, you two come with me. Frank, stay here, and Pat can start showing you the inside of the cab of a big rig.''

Frank didn't miss the sudden interest his brother was showing in Teri, and he smiled as Joe instantly struck up a conversation with her.

"Frank," said Pat, "hop up in the driver's seat, and I'll show you around."

Frank climbed up into the cab—and it *was* a climb. The seat was a good six feet off the ground, and Frank had to make his way up a series of metal rungs and footholds built into the cab wall. As he sat behind the wheel, he realized for the first time the wide view of the road a big rig driver has. On the dashboard in front of him was a bewildering collection of switches, knobs, dials, and lights.

Pat sat in the passenger seat. "Now, this particular truck has a standard or stick-shift transmission," she began. "You know what that means, right?"

Frank nodded. "It means you push in the clutch pedal to change gears." He tapped the pedal with his left foot.

"Right," said Pat. "Except in these rigs, you have to *double-clutch*—push the pedal once to get *out* of a gear and then again to get *into* the next one. Some trucks have automatic transmissions, but I don't care for them. Most truckers don't. Shifting is where we get one of the names we call ourselves—gearjammers. We do a lot of shifting. This truck has twelve forward gears. For the first six, you move the stick on the floor here, like this." She demonstrated the six gears. "And then you pull this lever and go through the same motions for gears seven through twelve.

"The cab is hooked to the trailer with what we call a fifth wheel—that big round thing you can see out the back window, there. See it? Okay. When you back this up into position in front of a trailer, a heavy pin in the trailer—the kingpin— locks into the notch in the wheel, and you're attached. Then you hook up a lot of cables and wires, so you can control the lights on the trailer from the cab. And the air brakes, too, of course."

"Whoa! Slow down a little," said Frank, holding up his hands. "I'm still trying to figure out twelve forward gears."

"Oh, don't worry, Frank," Pat told him. "You won't be driving an eighteen-wheeler for a long time yet." She pointed to some of the controls and gizmos and went on. "This light warns you if your fifth wheel connection is loose, and this shows the pressure in your air-brake cylinders. This toggle switch here controls—"

"Pat—"

"The safety lights. Over *here*—"

"Pat! Hold on a minute!"

"Am I going too fast?" she asked with a grin.

"Even airplane cockpits aren't as complicated as this," Frank said, shaking his head.

"Learning how to drive a truck like this one isn't like learning to drive your dad's car. It takes years to learn how, and a lot *more* years to get to be as good as I am."

"How long have you been at it?"

Pat laughed. "Never mind! Quite a while. I've got almost two million miles behind me, if you want to put it that way."

Frank whistled. "Two *million!*"

"Pat! Frank!"

Frank turned at the sound of the deep voice and saw that Matt was standing by his office door, motioning to them. "In here!"

Frank and Pat climbed down and went to the office. Joe was already there, standing beside Matt's desk.

"Ultratech has a shipment to go tomorrow," Matt told them. "The trailer will be loaded and ready by midafternoon. Pat, are you willing to take it out late tomorrow afternoon?"

She glanced at Frank. "Sure, if my helper is."

"I'm game."

Matt asked, "Got any ideas on how to keep the shipment from being swiped?"

Frank shrugged and thought a moment, then he asked, "Have all the trucks been stopped on deserted roads?"

"Yes."

"Will there be any deserted stretches tomorrow?"

Matt handed Pat a sheet of paper, which she studied for a moment before saying, "There are a few spots that are pretty deserted."

Frank met his brother's eyes. "If you and Tony could follow us in the van, we could keep in touch by CB. We might be able to trap this gang."

Joe nodded. "We'd have to stay far enough behind so we wouldn't be seen, but close enough to get to you fast if trouble happens. Maybe a mile behind you."

"Let's say two, just to be sure you won't be spotted. You could still get to us in a couple of minutes."

"Then what?" Matt asked, frowning. "Say there are four guys, like the other times. There'd be four of you against four of them. With the numbers even, how could you be sure they wouldn't get the shipment?"

"We figure the gang counts on overpowering a driver and getting away fast," Frank said. "The first time they run into organized resistance, they're likely to scatter. If we're lucky, we should be able to bag some of them. At the worst, we'll keep the shipment."

Matt didn't look convinced. "That's what you *think*, huh?"

"Right," Joe replied firmly. "That's what we're here to do, isn't it?"

"Well—okay," Matt finally said. "I just hope you—"

The door to Matt's office swung open, and Frank and Joe watched a man in jeans and a T-shirt stride in. He was tall and well-built, with reddish blond hair and a baseball cap pushed back on his head. His expression was angry and worried.

"What's this about Mike being in the hospital?" he demanded.

"You ought to knock, Hal," said Matt. "He's going to be all right."

"Matt, I told you *I* should be driving that Ultratech stuff!"

"Then you'd be in the hospital instead of Mike," Matt replied tersely. "Guys, meet Hal Brady, one of our drivers. Hal, Frank and Joe Hardy."

Frank stuck out a hand. "Glad to—"

Hal ignored him. "Well, I'm going to take the *next* shipment, right? Those creeps wouldn't take *my* truck, I can tell you that!"

"Pat's driving the next load, Hal," Matt told him. His tone left no room for argument.

Hal's face reddened, and his fists clenched at his sides. "Matt, this is crazy! A *woman* in a situation like this—"

"Don't worry about me. I can take care of myself," Pat snapped.

Frank looked over at Joe, who gave a slight

shake of the head. It was obvious his brother felt just as uncomfortable as he did.

Hal's voice rose. "Matt, you've got to—"

Matt cut him off, slamming his hand down on the desk with a loud thwack. "Enough! As long as I'm running this business, *I'm* making the decisions around here. And I say Pat is going to take that shipment!" His jaw was clenched tight, and veins in his neck stood out.

For a second Joe thought Hal might leap across the desk at Matt, but he just growled, "You won't *have* a business if you keep making dumb decisions like this." He turned and left the office.

There was silence for a moment. Finally Pat said, "Well, I've got to get some work done on that engine. Frank, see me when you're done here." Then she, too, was gone.

Frank and Joe were left in the office with Matt, who was staring stonily down at his desk.

"What did you make of this business with the rat out there?" Frank asked after a moment, trying to get back to the case. "If that was meant for you, then you're being warned. What's it about?"

Matt folded his arms across his chest. "It's nothing—not worth worrying about. Just one of a series of bad practical jokes someone's pulling on me—phone calls late at night, that kind of stuff. Probably someone I had to fire who has a grudge, that's all."

"But why did whoever it was leave the rat in the truck and not in your office?" Frank pressed. He wasn't convinced.

Matt shrugged. "Because they could sneak it into the truck easier than they could sneak it in here," he replied, sounding irritated. "They'd know that the message would get to me eventually."

"If you don't mind me asking," Joe said, "why *not* use Hal? He looks like he could handle himself pretty well in any situation."

"First of all," replied Matt, "Pat is every bit as good a driver as he is. Second, Hal has been giving me a hard time lately. Thinks he should be top driver around here, and I don't. Third—" He sighed and suddenly seemed very tired. "She is *family*. This gang is getting inside information somehow, and I hate not being able to trust my people, but—I have to go with family."

"Has Hal been with you long?" asked Frank.

"Five years," Matt answered. "Oh, he's not bad, but—"

The phone on Matt's desk rang. He picked it up. "Matt Simone . . . Yes . . . Right, we're taking it tomorrow afternoon. . . ." The voice on the other end went on for a while. Matt tried to speak at first, but then he gave up and just listened, a grim expression on his face.

"I understand," he said at last. "Yes, you made yourself very clear. Yes—we will, you can count on it. . . . Right." Then he slowly set the receiver into its cradle.

"That was the head honcho at Ultratech," Matt said. "I sure hope you guys know what you're doing, because if this truckload doesn't get through, Ultratech is going to find another shipping company—and that'll be the end of Lombard Hauling."

Chapter
6

FRANK AND JOE studied Matt's grim expression. "Somebody once said," Joe began, breaking the silence, " 'It ain't over till it's over.' Don't count Lombard out yet, Matt. It's our turn to call the shots."

Matt smiled wearily. "I just hope you boys know what you're doing."

The next day, by midafternoon, the Ultratech trailer had arrived, and Pat was backing her tractor up to hitch on. Her rig was a "cab-over," which meant that the motor was under the cab rather than in front under a hood. Frank watched as she expertly set the big machine in exactly the right place, then hopped out to see to the hookups.

"Before I go out on the road," she told Frank, "I want to be sure that everything is just the way it's supposed to be. Stick around and watch. You might learn something."

Joe, who would be following in the van with Tony, was excused to leave early. It would take another hour or two before they were ready to go, so Joe took the time to talk with Teri Yarnell. Going over to her desk, he saw that she was writing down columns of numbers in a ledger.

"Are you a relative of Matt's?" he asked her. "It seems like half the people here are."

"Not me," she said, smiling up at him. "But I feel like I might as well be. Everyone here is so nice. Mr. Simone is so sweet, except lately, and that's because he's been real worried. And Felix—Mr. Kinney—well, he's been teaching me how to use the computer. He's very patient, and he says that once I know how to use it, I can take some courses and get a better job somewhere else. Although I don't know—I think I'd rather stay here."

"But if you could get a better job—"

"The thing is," she said, giving Joe a serious look, "a better job might mean longer hours, and I don't know if I want to spend so much time at a job. I mean, Mr. Simone works long hours. And Felix—well, it seems like he spends most of his evenings here lately, working with that computer."

"Doesn't leave much time for having fun, huh?" said Joe. "I guess your boyfriend wouldn't like it if you worked evenings."

"No, he sure wouldn't," said Teri.

Joe tried not to look disappointed but didn't quite succeed, and Teri seemed to suppress a giggle.

"If I *had* a boyfriend, that is," she added, closing the ledger.

Joe shot her a big smile. "Well, since you don't, and since you don't have to spend your evenings at a job . . ."

He was interrupted when Felix Kinney stuck his head out of his office. "Teri, come in here, will you?"

"Be right there," she called. Then, turning back to Joe, she smiled and said, "Well—I'd better go. See you later."

"You can count on it," Joe replied.

Frank was astonished at how many details Pat dealt with before the truck was ready for the road. Every coupling, electrical system, and warning light had to be tested twice. She checked the brake cylinders, hoses, the eighteen huge tires, the oil and other fluids. Most important, Pat told him, was the way the trailer's cargo was stored and fastened down.

"If your cargo isn't tied down tight, or if it isn't balanced right, you could have some real trouble." She went through the trailer, tugging at the straps that held the stacked cartons in place on their wooden pallets. "These electronics could get damaged, or even worse, you could lose control of your rig. That's never happened to me, and it won't happen this trip, either. But the only way to be sure is to check it all out yourself."

Finally, late in the afternoon, she was satisfied and told Frank to climb aboard. He watched curiously as Pat made some involved maneuvers with the pedals, gearshift, and steering wheel. The big diesel engine under their seats roared to life, and they slowly pulled away from Lombard Hauling. They were on the road.

A couple of hours later, when they were moving smoothly along a stretch of interstate highway, Frank called Joe on their prearranged CB channel.

"This is Big Brother calling Tailend Charlie. Do you read me, Tailend Charlie? Over."

There was some crackly static on the line, but Joe's voice could be heard over it. "This is Tailend Charlie, back at you. You're coming through, but there's some interference, over."

"We passed Exit Thirty-four a couple of miles back, are you in position? Over."

"Big Brother, we are just coming up to Exit Thirty-four now, we will close up the gap a little, over."

"I copy that. Big Brother over and out."

The truck raced through the fading light. "When will we get there?" asked Frank.

"This is a short run. We should pull in at

about midnight," answered Pat. "Unless we have an unscheduled delay, that is."

From the passenger seat, Frank sat and gazed out at the flat country dotted with factories and industrial parks. Soon the land they passed through was even less developed, and the traffic thinned out to almost nothing. It was nearly dark, and Pat had turned on all her lights. "We take the next exit," she said. "We'll be on a surface road for a while."

"Why not just use the interstates?" asked Frank.

"Because this way is shorter, takes less time and less gas. That way we keep our cost down. Otherwise, some other trucker would underbid us."

As she turned on her directional signal, she added, "Better make sure your friends know we're getting off here."

Frank picked up the CB microphone. "This is Big Brother calling Tailend Charlie, are you there? Over."

"This is Charlie, over," came Joe's voice. The interference was worse now.

"We're getting off at Exit Fourteen, do you copy? Over."

"Roger, Big Brother. Over and out."

There was almost no traffic, and Frank wondered whether any of the occasional headlights he saw belonged to someone who wanted to hijack their truck.

Pat must have picked up on his uneasiness. Even though she kept her eyes on the road, she said, "Take it easy, Frank. It'll happen if and when it happens."

"Sure," said Frank, "but this just strikes me as a great spot to do it, that's all."

"Could be," she said, "but—" She suddenly stared into the rearview mirror. "There are some headlights coming up real fast behind us, Frank. Grab that CB!"

Frank did. "This is Big Brother. Stand by. We may have company. Over."

The noisy static over the little speaker was much worse, and Joe's voice could be heard only in snatches. ". . . your position . . . we are . . . keep us . . ."

"Tailend Charlie, your signal is breaking up, I can hardly hear you at all, over." Frank's voice was urgent.

A big, bulky step van pulled out directly in front of them from a side road and slowed to a crawl. Pat turned the wheel abruptly, and her truck swerved to the left. She tried to swing around the van, but it shot forward and continued to stay ahead of them. Then it slowed again as another vehicle pulled up beside Pat's rig. This was a large, powerful tow truck, the kind used to tow eighteen-wheelers. It swung its nose against the Lombard rig and tried to force it over onto the shoulder.

"This is it," said Pat. "Hang on, Frank, we're in for a rough ride!"

"Tailend Charlie, do you copy?" said Frank urgently into the CB mike. "This is Big Brother, and we have bad company. Come and get us, over."

Pat turned the wheel and bumped the tow truck, sending it swerving out into the left lane. An oncoming car headed for the shoulder of the road, horn blaring, and then disappeared behind them.

"I'll hold these guys off as long as I can," said Pat. She wrestled with the steering wheel, her feet moving rapidly on the gas, brake, and clutch pedals. "But I hope Joe and Tony are nearby."

Frank fiddled with the CB. "I don't hear them. There's some kind of glitch in the CB. I don't know, they might be picking up our signal just fine—"

He collided with the dashboard as Pat banged into the rear of the bulky step van in front of them. The impact forced Pat to drop her speed. Meanwhile the tow truck continued to hem them in on the left side. Again Pat rammed the step van, and there was a solid thunk. This time Frank was ready and he braced himself with his arms.

The van pulled ahead slightly, but then its brake lights glowed as it slowed still more.

Pat shook her head. "That van has some kind of reinforced back bumper. If we hit it too hard, in a cab-over like this, we could total our engine, maybe even turn over. I'm going to have to stop."

Again Frank spoke into the mike. "This is Big Brother calling Tailend Charlie. It is going down, right now. If you read me, join the party, over."

He heard only static over the speaker.

Pat pulled onto the right shoulder and stopped. The step van stopped right in front of the rig, and the tow truck parked behind them. Frank tried to keep cool as he checked out the window and sideview mirror. The doors to both vehicles opened, and two men got out of each. Two carried baseball bats, one had a tire iron, and one had a long, heavy crowbar. All four wore ski masks. They moved menacingly toward the big truck.

Chapter

7

"Is your door locked?" Frank asked Pat as the four masked toughs split up and approached the truck's cab, two on each side.

"Yes, for whatever good it'll do," she said.

"Come on, open up, lady!" yelled one of the bandits, swinging his bat close to the window. Pat didn't react.

"Joe and Tony ought to be here any second," whispered Frank. "If we can hold them off for a minute or so—"

"Once they get to smashing windows, we'll be lucky to have a minute," Pat said. Frank saw her staring nervously down at the two large men on her side, and he didn't blame her for being scared.

Suddenly there was a loud clang of metal striking metal on Frank's side of the cab. Spinning around in his seat, he saw a hijacker swing his crowbar into the metalwork of the cab just below his door.

"Open up, kid!" he called. "You know what we want. Make it easy on yourself and don't give us any trouble."

"Sorry, but I'm not allowed to talk to strangers," Frank called out.

"Oh, a wise punk, huh?" called the goon. He angrily climbed up toward Frank's door, raising his heavy bar to smash it into the window.

As he did, Frank opened the door and kicked it with his right leg, catching the man in the mask unprepared and knocking him to the ground. Quickly he slammed the door closed again and locked it.

Pat screamed as a baseball bat whacked loudly against the safety glass in her window, cracking it with a cobweb pattern. One more shot from the bat would shatter it. She tried what Frank had done on his side, using the door itself to jar the intruder loose. But her guy grabbed the door handle and tossed his bat down, catching hold of Pat's left arm. He pulled hard and managed to drag her halfway out of her seat.

Frank snatched up a large, heavy flashlight from the tool compartment behind his seat and brought it down hard on the man's hand. The hijacker yelled and let go of Pat's arm, but he still hung on to the door. Pat pulled on it but couldn't close it. Out of the corner of his eye, Frank saw another hood appear in his window, tire iron poised to strike.

A horn blared and headlights suddenly lit up the whole scene. Frank let out a sigh of relief as the black van screeched to a stop within a few feet of the action, and Joe and Tony jumped out.

Frank watched Joe leap for the tough who was hanging on to the driver's side door and fling him to the pavement.

Meanwhile, Tony, holding a bat of his own, rushed around the front of the rig. He feinted and dodged one big goon, then hit the guy holding the tire iron behind the knee with his bat, so that the guy suddenly dropped out of Frank's line of vision.

Frank knew that the momentum had shifted. Opening his door, he dropped lightly to the ground, shouting for Pat to do the same.

"Let's get out of here!" came a shrill cry from one of the ski masks. The four men made a rush for their vehicles, two limping badly. The tow truck started to roar away, burning rubber, as its passenger dived for the seat and closed the door. Tony tried tackling one of the remaining two, but the beefy man shook him off and joined his buddy in the step van. That, too, took off fast, leaving the Hardys, Tony, and Pat standing in the quiet nighttime road.

"Should we go after them?" asked Joe.

"I don't think it'd be too hot an idea," Frank

replied. "We had the element of surprise working for us just now, but who knows what they'll have waiting for us next. For now, let's just be satisfied that this hijacking didn't work."

"Hey, guys, I got the license number on that tow truck!" Tony shouted, his face still flushed from the excitement of the brief action. "That would help us nail them, right?"

Joe slapped Tony on the back. "Write it down, Tony. Nice work."

Pat smiled at her three guards. "You did a fine job on those apes. Maybe they'll think twice before going after a Lombard truck again."

"Maybe," Frank answered. "But if they do think twice, they might just be better prepared next time. Let's get back on the road."

"Tell you what," said Pat. "Why don't you head back to Bayport with Tony and your brother. I can take this baby the rest of the way. It's just a short hop."

"You sure, Pat?" Joe asked doubtfully.

"I'm sure. That bunch won't try anything again tonight. Go on back and tell Matt what happened. He's waiting to hear from us, and he's overdue for some good news. I'll be back tomorrow."

They said good night, and with Tony now in the backseat behind the Hardys, Joe turned the van around and started back.

As they drove, Tony spoke up. "It seemed to me like the guys we ran into the other day—you know, at that warehouse—might have been two of these guys.''

Frank glanced back and said, "There are a lot of ski masks around, Tony."

"Yeah," Tony agreed. "But the guy who ran over me in the warehouse sure felt about the same size and shape as the one I grabbed tonight."

"I wouldn't be surprised if you're right," Joe said, studying Tony in the rearview mirror. "There are so many connections between what went down there and what's happening to Lombard Hauling." He sighed. "I wish Matt would open up to us more. Tony, do you know why he won't bring the law into this?"

"He's afraid that someone in the family—"

"That's part of it," Frank said. "But I think there's more to it than your uncle's letting on. Let's get over there now. Maybe he'll still be there, and maybe he'll be ready to level with us."

"Let's hope Dad got some information on Mickey Vane and the owners of the warehouse," said Joe.

"And don't forget to check out who owns that tow truck," insisted Tony.

They drove the rest of the way in silence. The excitement of the fight with the hijackers had worn off, and they all felt exhausted. As they pulled up in front of Lombard, Joe noticed that the office lights were on.

"Great!" he said. "Matt is still here. He must

be waiting for news on the shipment. Let's give him the good word and try to pump him for a little more information.''

As the three boys were walking toward the office, they suddenly heard something.

"Listen!" Frank said.

Loud voices were coming from Matt's office, as were thumps and banging sounds.

"Sounds like furniture is being thrown around," Joe said, a frown creasing his forehead.

He broke into a run, with the other two just behind him. But before he reached the office door, it flew open, and a pale and frightened Felix Kinney ran out.

He spotted the boys and raced up to them, wringing his hands.

"You've got to stop them!" he yelled. "Stop them *right now*. They're going to kill each other!"

Frank raced ahead and reached the door a split second before Joe. Flinging it open, he saw Matt Simone and Hal Brady battling inside. They couldn't move much in the cramped office, but Matt had the driver in a headlock, and Hal was landing chopping punches on Matt's stomach. Both men were breathing heavily. Furniture was knocked over, and papers were strewn on the floor.

Tony dodged past the Hardys, grabbed his uncle's arm, and tried to pull him away. "Uncle Matt, cut it out! Come on, this is crazy!"

Matt shook him off and dived back at Hal.

Frank and Joe exchanged a quick look, then leaped into action. Each grabbing hold of a fighter, they dragged them apart. After a moment's struggle the three boys were able to separate Matt and Hal. The two men stood gasping for air. There was a cut at the corner of Matt's mouth, Frank noticed, and Hal was going to have a black eye.

"Get your gear together and get out of here," growled Matt when he'd caught his breath. "You're fired!"

"Fired, huh?" Hal glared at his boss. "Before I'm through, you won't have a company to fire anybody from!"

Chapter

8

HAL STALKED OUT of the office, slamming the door behind him.

"What started *that?*" Tony demanded.

Matt wouldn't discuss it, other than to say, "*Nobody* tells me how to run my business."

Focusing first on Tony, then on Joe and Frank, he suddenly exclaimed, "Hey, what are you guys doing back here? Where's Pat? What happened to the truck?"

Frank quickly explained about the hijack attempt, and how it had been stopped cold. "Pat said she could make it the rest of the way without an escort. She ought to be there within an hour. Score one for the good guys."

Matt sat in his desk chair and let out a long,

slow breath. "Oh, boy. You just took a big load off my mind."

Leaning forward, Joe said, "Matt, we need to talk some more."

Matt held up a hand. "Not tonight, okay? It's late, very late, we're all tired, and I want to close up here and go home. You should, too."

Joe frowned, but he knew Matt had a point. They'd all had a rough day. Saying good night, he, Frank, and Tony went out to the van. As they walked, Felix joined them.

"Thanks for stepping in back there," Felix told them. "They've both got such tempers, and they're too big for me—I couldn't have separated them if I'd tried."

Joe paused and faced Felix. "What's the story between those two?" he asked. "Do you know?"

Felix shook his head sadly. "Not really. Oh, I know that there's been trouble brewing for a while, a lot of bad feeling, but I don't know why. Matt won't say, although he usually talks to me about his business problems."

"You put in long hours," Frank observed.

"Not always," Felix replied with a wan smile. "But sometimes things just pile up. Well, good night. See you tomorrow."

As they drove toward Tony's house, with Frank behind the wheel, Joe said, "How does Hal Brady look as an inside member of a gang? He seems to have it in for Matt. That might be a motive."

"Could be," Frank said. "We'll check him

out, find out if he has a record or anything." He flicked his gaze up to the rearview mirror. "Meanwhile, there's been a pair of headlights behind us ever since we left Lombard. I want to see if it's a coincidence."

He made a complicated series of turns, keeping an eye on the mirror the whole time. After a few minutes he said, "They're still on our tail."

"Lose 'em," said Joe. He called out to Tony in the backseat, "I hope your seat belt is fastened."

The van was equipped with a supercharged engine, and Frank floored the gas pedal, throwing the three of them back against their seats. They raced away from the trailing car, but it sped up, taking a sharp right turn with a squeal of tires as it tried to stay with the Hardys' van.

Frank had studied high performance driving. He knew just how fast the van could corner and when to downshift drifting into a tight curve. As he roared along, missing curbs and hydrants by a hairbreadth, the pursuing headlights gradually lost ground. After some more maneuvers, the gap grew to a couple of hundred yards.

Frank downshifted, swung sharply into an unlit alley, and turned off the van's lights. A moment later whoever had been following them went speeding past—in a large, powerful tow truck.

"Was that the one those hijackers had?" Tony asked.

"Either that," said Joe, "or an exact copy.

But if it *was* the same guys, at least we know they didn't go after Pat and the truck again.''

They waited a few minutes to make sure the tow truck would not reappear.

"We shook them," Frank said.

Joe yawned. "Let's call it a night. We'll be short on sleep as it is."

Frank nodded. He pulled back out into the street, dropped Tony off at his house, and then drove home. By the time he had pulled into the driveway and he and Joe were out and locking the doors of the van, Frank was yawning, too. He felt exhausted and ready to catch what sleep he could.

He came instantly alert, however, as a heavy-duty motor sounded in the night. Spinning around quickly, he saw a hulking tow truck pull across the entrance to their driveway. Behind it was a large step van, which stopped at the curb.

Two men got out of each vehicle and spread out. They were masked and carried heavy lengths of pipe.

Slowly they began to close in.

Chapter

9

FRANK AND JOE set themselves back to back.

"Hi, there!" Frank said brightly. "You know, guys, we have to stop meeting like this."

The tallest of the four—was it the guy Tony had hit behind the knees earlier that evening? Joe wondered—spoke. His voice was a throaty whisper.

"You two been messing with the wrong people. You got a lesson to learn about minding other people's business."

"Folks keep telling me I'm a slow learner," Joe said. He shifted his eyes and his weight as the men moved closer.

The hood closest to the van was short and broad with a barrel chest. "Oh, a wise guy!" he said in a rough, nasal voice. "How'd you like some body work on your wheels, wise guy?"

He turned and, gripping his pipe with both hands, he slammed it into the black surface of the van's rear door.

There was a harsh metallic crunch, and suddenly an earsplitting horn went off, filling the quiet night air. Up and down the street, lights went on in houses and the shadows of faces appeared in windows.

The taller goon snapped, "You moron, you set off their car alarm! Let's get out of here!"

"Leaving so soon?" asked Frank. "But we were just getting to know you."

The short, squat goon took a step toward Frank, pipe raised, before the taller guy yelled, "Move it, you idiot! The cops could show up any minute!"

They ran for their trucks, but the one who had hit the van turned back and shouted, "Next time you won't be so lucky, wise guy!"

Fenton Hardy came running out of the house in his robe as the gang barreled down the street and around the corner. Frank shut the alarm off. When he, Joe, and their father went inside, they found Mrs. Hardy in the living room, sleepy and worried.

"What's the matter?" she asked.

"Nothing, Mom," replied Joe. "Some prowlers set off the alarm. Everything's under control."

Fenton turned to his wife. "I'm just going to talk to Frank and Joe for a few minutes."

Mrs. Hardy sighed. "The only thing worse for

your sleep than being married to a detective is having them for children!'' she exclaimed. But there was a smile on her face when she left the room.

After settling down in Fenton's office, Frank and Joe told him of the day's events, up to the getaway of the gang moments before.

"It sounds as though those guys meant business," Fenton said. He let out a low whistle, then added, "Well, I have information for you. The warehouse is owned by a big outfit that has properties all over Bayport and rents them out through a realty office. That place was rented to an outfit called United Sales, Inc. They paid three months' rent in advance with a cashier's check.

"It turns out that United Sales is a phony. The address they gave is an empty lot, and the phone number doesn't exist. The man who handled the rental says he didn't check out the address because he knew the cashier's check was good. He *might* be able to recognize the guy who gave him the check, but he doubts it. As far as this part of your investigation goes, it looks like a dead end."

"How about Mickey Vane?" asked Frank.

Fenton shrugged. "A small-time hood, with a few convictions for assault and breaking and entering. He was once investigated for his supposed involvement in labor racketeering, but there wasn't any solid evidence. When he could, he got jobs driving trucks, but they never lasted long. Either he'd quit or get fired. Lombard Hauling hired him two years back and fired him five months later, so Matt's story checks out.

"Are you ruling Matt out as a possible suspect?" asked Fenton.

Frank looked at his brother. "My gut feeling is that he couldn't be involved," he said, "but I can't be absolutely certain."

"Well, *I'm* certain," said Joe. "He's not part of the gang. What could he gain?"

"Anything's possible," Frank countered. "Maybe his business was going under anyway, and he's working an insurance scam—you know, burn the place down, destroy the trucks, and then blame unknown villains while collecting the insurance."

Joe stared at him. "Oh, come on—"

"Okay, so it's a long shot, but it's possible. Maybe that's why he doesn't want the police brought in. Maybe he hired us because he hoped we couldn't do the job."

"Well, I like Hal Brady a lot better as a bad guy," Joe said emphatically. "He's more the type."

"Who's Hal Brady?" asked Fenton.

"He's a driver at Lombard," explained Frank. "He and Matt don't get along. They had a big fight tonight, and Matt fired him."

"*And,*" Joe put in, "he made a threat as he was leaving. Something like 'You won't have a business when I'm through with you.'"

"Could you find out if he's got a record?" Frank asked his father.

"I suppose I can. Any other suspects at the moment?"

"We haven't talked to everyone who works at Lombard yet," said Joe, "but I don't think we've eliminated anyone, really. Except for Pat Mulvaney and Matt," he added, giving his brother a defiant look.

"And Teri Yarnell, of course," Frank shot back, giving Joe a teasing smile.

"Right. And Teri Yarnell," Joe echoed. Seeing a questioning look on his father's face, he explained, "She's a girl who does office work there."

"And she's pretty, so she couldn't be involved in anything *criminal*," said Frank. "Right, Joe?"

"My *instincts* tell me that she's not a criminal," Joe said with mock indignation.

"Anyway," Frank said, getting back to the Lombard case, "we can be pretty sure there's some kind of connection between the warehouse that was selling stolen Ultratech products and what's been going down at Lombard."

"And the killing of Mickey Vane," added Joe. "But why was he killed? And why did they shut that warehouse operation down so suddenly?"

"Let's see what we can find out," Frank said, stifling a yawn as he got up and stretched. "In the morning, that is."

"Oh, Dad," Joe said as he got up, too. He handed his father a piece of paper. "Could you run a check on this license plate number for us? It was used by this gang tonight."

"Chances are it was stolen," Frank said. "That's the way these types usually work."

"I'll look into it," Fenton promised. "And— one more thing. This gang didn't need to follow you tonight to know where you live, so keep watching your backs. They may know what you're really doing down there."

"Don't worry, Dad," said Joe. "We'll take care of ourselves."

His father gave him a tired smile. "Well, it's too late for me to start worrying now."

The next morning when Frank and Joe reported for work, they saw Teri Yarnell alone in Felix Kinney's office. Joe walked in to say hello.

"Where's Felix?" he asked her.

"When he works late at night, he comes in a little late the next morning," she answered. She studied him for a minute. "I've been thinking about you."

Joe smiled. "What a coincidence. I've been thinking about you, too."

"No, really. I can't help wondering—what are you doing here?"

Joe suddenly felt uncomfortable. "Doing? I'm working here. Just like you."

"Yes, but why?"

"To earn money." Joe didn't like telling Teri something less than the truth, but he knew that he didn't have a choice. "I don't get it. What's so strange about working here?"

She shrugged. "I don't know exactly. You and your brother don't seem like the kind of guys who go to work at this kind of place, that's all."

"Well," Joe said, hoping he sounded convincing, "we *are* working at this kind of place." He grabbed a chair and pulled it over beside hers. "And you know, it has its advantages."

"You think so?"

"Right now I definitely think so," said Joe.

"Joe! Frank! In my office!" Joe recognized Matt Simone's voice even before he turned to see the tall, muscular man. Reluctantly, he stood up.

"One of these days we'll have a chance to finish a conversation," he told Teri.

"I'll look forward to it," she said, giving Joe a warm smile as he walked out of the room. Matt waved Frank and Joe to chairs in his office, and then sat down behind his desk. "We have a special order from Ultratech to go out today," he told them. "Pat is headed back with the empty truck—what we call deadheading. In the meantime we'll load up a trailer with stock we have in storage here. Frank, you ride with Pat, and Joe and Tony can follow, like yesterday. That okay with you?"

"Sure," replied Joe. "If it's all right with Tony."

"He'll be over here by noon," Matt replied. "I figure that—"

The office door opened and Hal Brady came

in, followed by a short, stocky man Joe recognized as Lou Gerard, the union manager he and Frank had seen at the office two days before.

"Simone, you fired this man without cause," said Gerard, an angry look on his face. "Our contract doesn't allow it. You have to take him back."

"There was plenty of cause," Matt retorted. "He was giving me nothing but trouble and making threats. I still run this outfit!"

Gerard leaned over Matt's desk, and said, "Simone, either you put him back on the payroll—today—or I pull every union employee out of here right now. Every driver and every mechanic."

Felix Kinney had come in behind the others, and now he spoke up. "He's right, Matt. You didn't have enough grounds to get rid of him. We can't afford to have a walkout, and you know it."

Matt glared at Gerard and Brady but then nodded. "Okay. You win. But I *can* suspend him, and that's what I'm going to do. Go home for the rest of the week, Brady. And remember, *I* call the shots around here."

Brady wheeled around and was gone. Lou Gerard stayed where he was. "We still have to talk, Simone."

"We have nothing to talk about, Lou. Beat it, I've got work to do."

Gerard turned and called out the door, "Turk! Get in here!"

A barrel-chested man with a flattened nose appeared in the doorway. "Yes, sir, Mr. Gerard?"

Matt fixed Gerard with an icy glare. "Listen, Brady is back on the payroll. That's all you and I had to talk about. Take a hike, and take your gorilla with you."

Gerard slowly shook his head and said to the man in the doorway, "Let's go, Turk. Mr. Simone doesn't want us to talk." His voice was mocking, falsely polite.

"That's too bad, Mr. Gerard. People ought to talk to people," Turk replied.

Joe jerked his head around when Turk spoke and studied the beefy guy more closely. Turk returned his look with a flat stare.

"Yeah, it is," said Gerard. "Come on. Drive me back to the office." He looked back at Matt. "We'll see you around, Mr. Simone."

Matt left the office to make sure Gerard and his driver were really leaving. After he was gone, Joe leaned over to Frank and said quietly, "Did you notice anything about that guy Turk?"

"Just that he looked and sounded like an old boxer who's taken too many punches," Frank answered.

"Right," agreed Joe. "He also sounded like one of the guys who was wearing a ski mask last night. The one who smashed our van with a pipe."

Chapter
10

FRANK STARED AT his brother in amazement.
"Are you sure this guy Turk was one of *those*
guys?"

"Pretty sure. I remember that voice. He's the
right size and shape, too."

Before Frank could ask Joe anything more,
Matt returned to the office. "Sorry about that,"
he told them, sitting back down at his desk. "I
just wanted to make sure those two went straight
out of here."

Frank gave Matt a probing look and said, "It
might make things a lot easier for us if you could
tell us what's been happening between you and
this Lou Gerard, Matt."

Matt still refused to respond to Frank's question. Changing the subject, he said, "You two

can help get that trailer loaded with the Ultratech stock. We're on a tight schedule.''

Before Frank or Joe could argue further, Matt had picked up a phone and begun to dial. Catching his brother's eye, Frank signaled that they might as well leave.

Once they were outside the office, Joe grabbed Frank's arm. ''We can't just let this go, Frank. We have to make Matt tell us about Lou Gerard. If we tie Turk into the hijackings, and he works for Gerard—''

''Maybe his work for Gerard has nothing to do with the hijacking,'' Frank suggested. He was frustrated, too, but he knew they wouldn't get anywhere jumping to conclusions. ''Maybe he has a straight job for the union, and hijacking is just a sideline.''

''And maybe Gerard is in it up to his neck,'' Joe shot back.

''But what would Gerard's motive be in all this?'' Frank asked. ''He works for the union local, right? Putting Lombard out of business puts some of his people out of work. It doesn't figure.''

''No. Something is missing, you're right about that, Frank. That's exactly why Matt has to open up. Let's go back and—''

Joe paused, hearing Felix call to him and Frank from the loading dock.

''We have to get that trailer filled and ready to go. Give us a hand, guys, we're fighting the clock here.''

As they walked over, Frank said quietly, "Okay, Joe. We'll talk to Matt soon, and we won't take no for an answer."

As the wooden pallets stacked with Ultratech equipment were piled aboard the trailer, Pat pulled her tractor in, backed into place, and hitched up the fifth wheel. While she started her lengthy predrive check, Frank tapped Joe on the shoulder.

"Now's as good a time as any. Let's talk to Matt."

When they entered his office again, Matt looked up from some paperwork. "What's up, guys?"

"Matt," said Joe. "If we're going to do the job right for you, we need your cooperation."

Matt frowned. "Listen, I've tried to be cooperative. I—"

Frank interrupted. "You're stonewalling us, Matt. There are things you won't talk to us about that could be important pieces of this puzzle. You may think you've got good reason to keep things to yourself—"

"I've told you about everything that relates to these hijackings," insisted Matt.

"You mean, everything you *think* relates to the hijackings," replied Frank. "We don't have to agree with you."

Joe began firing off questions. "Number one. Why do you refuse to bring in the police? Your company is about to go under, and you won't take the most obvious step to protect it. Number two. How did the trouble start between you and

Hal Brady? Number three. What's the deal with Lou Gerard?"

Matt began to protest. "That stuff has nothing to do with—"

"Matt, you don't know that for sure," Frank cut in. "We have reason to think you're wrong. Now, you want us to do something, but we can't—unless you level with us. You know that anything you tell us is strictly confidential."

"Anyway," Joe went on, "here's the bottom line. Either you talk to us and give us the facts we need to do the job right, or we'll have to quit. We can't work when our hands are tied."

Matt stared first at Joe and then at Frank. It was clear that he hadn't expected a confrontation. "You two serious about this?"

"Joe speaks for both of us," Frank replied. "What's it going to be?"

Matt held up his hands. "Okay, okay. You win. Look, I'll tell you what. We don't have time to do it right now. As soon as you get back from this haul, we'll sit down and I'll tell you anything you want to know. Good enough?"

"Good enough," Frank answered.

"Okay, then. Good luck on this trip, guys."

Shortly after noon Pat and Frank were on their way in the big rig, with Joe and Tony a couple of miles behind in the van. It was exactly the same setup as on the previous day.

"Where are we headed?" asked Frank.

"There's a map in the glove compartment with the route marked out," Pat said. "These components are going to a distribution center west of here, some outfit that delivers to a big chain of electronics stores. Never been there before."

Frank checked in with Joe on the CB radio. Reception was clear this time, and Joe confirmed that the van was in place.

"You think that bunch will try to stop us again?" Pat asked.

"Sooner or later, they will," replied Frank. "It could be this trip."

"Well, I bet they don't, not today. They need more time to regroup," she said.

"I hope you're right," Frank told her. He scanned the road ahead, vaguely aware of something not being quite right. The voice of experience was whispering that Pat would lose her bet. He felt restless, edgy.

"Anyway, if they do hit us, we can take care of them. Right, Frank? Just like the first time."

"We'll give it our best shot," he told her. "Just remember, we won't have the element of surprise going for us. Now they'll be expecting you to have escorts."

After a while they turned from a heavily traveled surface road onto a less busy one that went out into open country. Frank called Joe and told him they were turning. The van was still two miles behind them. Keeping his eyes on the road ahead, Frank was searching for possible ambush sites. There seemed to be an awful lot of them.

"Uh-oh, what's this?" said Pat, slowing the truck down. Up ahead were brightly colored traffic barriers, topped by blinking amber lights. In front of the roadblock, a Day-Glo orange sign said Detour, and beneath it an arrow pointed down a road to the right. Beyond the barriers, the road disappeared around a curve.

Pat took the right turn indicated by the arrow. "Must be repairs or maybe an accident," she mumbled.

The new road went up a slight grade and then became steeper. They went through a series of S-curves and found themselves climbing hills that were getting higher and higher.

An alarm bell went off in Frank's mind.

"Pat," he said, twisting around nervously. "Hold it a second. I think this could be the—"

Just then she rounded a curve and hit the brakes, hard. No more than a hundred feet in front of them, a tree lay across the road. It completely blocked their way.

Frank grabbed the CB microphone. "Come in, Tailender," he said urgently. "I think we have trouble, a little way past the detour—"

As he spoke, he saw the dense undergrowth beside the road part. Two men came out. As on the night before, they wore ski masks. But this time, instead of clubs, they carried guns.

Chapter

11

FRANK WANTED TO WARN Joe and Tony about the hijackers having guns, but one of the toughs pointed his automatic straight at him.

"Put the mike down," he shouted. "Now."

Frank obeyed.

"Climb down from there." The speaker was the one Frank assumed was the leader, the tallest member of the gang. "No funny stuff this time. We'll just wait until your friends show up."

Pat glanced across at Frank, as though she expected him to have some kind of plan and wanted to know what it was.

"Just do what they tell you," he said quietly. "Don't make waves."

They climbed down, and Pat surveyed the winding, narrow road they were on. "You're going to have a tough time taking this rig down to the main road," she said.

The second gunman laughed. "Who says we're gonna do that, lady?"

"Shut up!" barked the first man. "Don't get sociable with these two. Or their friends. Just do your job."

A moment later the van appeared, with Joe at the wheel. Joe thought Tony might try taking the bad guys on, so he reached out to stop him.

"Not against guns, Tony. That would be a bad move. Be cool, all right?"

Tony nodded, but he glared at the gunmen as he climbed out of the van.

The other two members of the gang now drove up in a pickup truck. The traffic barriers and signs were now loaded in the back of the truck. One of the two walked up to the group of prisoners and stood in front of Frank.

"Hello again, wise guy."

Although the man wore a mask, Frank recognized his short, barrel-chested build immediately. He resisted the impulse to reply, "Hello, Turk," knowing that if he did so, it would be the end of him—and of Joe, Tony, and Pat. He remained silent.

"Stay and cover them," the head man called over to Turk. "Let's get busy."

Two of the gang members wrestled with the

fallen tree, lugging it to one side of the road. The leader knelt down and went under the rig, where he started fiddling with the hookups between tractor and trailer.

"Can you tell what he's doing?" Frank whispered to Pat.

Pat nodded, suddenly looking pale and frightened. "He-he's cutting the hoses," she whispered back. "The ones that run from the cab to the trailer's air brakes. But there's a backup safety system. It cuts in whenever the regular air brakes fail. It's automatic, unless—"

She stopped as the tall masked man moved to the back of the trailer, having finished with the hoses up front. There he went to work with a small acetylene torch and a hacksaw.

"Oh, no," she whispered, biting her lip.

"What? What's going on?" asked Joe.

"That guy, whoever he is, knows trucks. He's wrecking the cylinders, so the backup brake system won't work, either. But I don't understand! They won't be able to drive the rig in that condition!"

"Cut the chatter!" ordered the short goon who was guarding them.

Climbing out from under the trailer, the boss of the operation now called the two who had been moving the tree. They had succeeded in shoving it over enough to clear a narrow passage on the road.

"Lose the van," he said.

A gunman got into the Hardys' van and started it, then drove into the undergrowth beside the road, where it would be hidden from anyone driving by.

"Check the brakes," the second hood was told. Climbing into the cab of the truck, he got in the driver's seat and started the engine. He checked the readings on a couple of dials.

"Pressure is all the way down to zero," he called.

Joe had been watching their progress with a sinking feeling in the pit of his stomach. Suddenly he realized that with the boss's attention focused on the truck, there was only a single guard to contend with, the one he assumed was Turk. He flicked a glance at Frank, and his brother's slight nod showed that he agreed that this was their best chance to turn things around.

Joe saw Frank barely shift his eyes. Frank was signaling that he would go for the gun. Joe lay three fingers flat on his leg—go in three seconds.

Their sudden leap was perfectly coordinated. Joe hit the unsuspecting Turk just below the knees and drove him back and down. Frank wrenched the automatic pistol loose from his grasp. The maneuver worked perfectly.

Before Frank could move with the gun, however, a snarling voice came at him from behind.

"Turn around—slow, and hold it right there!"

Frank saw that the hood who had been moving the van had finished his task and was now standing next to Pat Mulvaney, with his automatic pointed at her head.

"Put the gun down, or she gets it first," he said, cocking the gun with a threatening click.

There was nothing else to do. Frank dropped the gun and raised his hands. Joe did the same.

Turk jumped to his feet and pulled Frank around roughly by the shoulder.

"You asked for this, wise guy," he said in his raspy voice. He drew back his right fist, but before he could throw the punch, Turk's arm was seized in an iron grip by the leader.

"Cut it out," said the bigger man. "You shouldn't have let them jump you. Now, let's get this over with, and try not to foul anything else up. And *you*"—he pointed a finger first at Frank, then at Joe—"any more dumb stunts and we'll shoot the four of you and leave you right here. Don't think we won't."

"We know you would," replied Joe. "But you can't blame us for trying."

The gang marched their four prisoners over to where the Lombard truck stood.

"You and you," said the boss, pointing to Joe and Tony, "in the sleeping compartment. Come on, move it!"

As in most long-distance trucks, the space behind the seats in Pat's rig was big enough to hold a small bed. A driver on a long haul could pull over and crawl in for a few hours' rest, or one of a team of drivers could catch some sleep while the other drove.

Tony and Joe were a tight fit in the compartment. Handcuffs were used to fasten them securely to stanchions in the frame of the cab. Frank was forced into the right-hand seat and cuffed to the inside door handle. Finally, Pat was led at gunpoint to the driver's seat and shackled to the steering wheel.

One of the gang climbed up on the driver's side and shoved into the seat beside Pat, keeping the door open. The head man got up on the right side. His automatic was trained on the four prisoners in the cab.

The hood in the driver's seat started the truck. Slowly he drove it forward, climbing up a fairly steep grade. Eventually the road leveled off and made a bend. Frank saw that the road was beginning to descend the hill, twisting and turning, clinging to a sheer rise on the right side. To the left of the road was a steep drop. Some of the turns were very sharp.

The masked driver revved up the engine to build up some momentum. But before the rig could build up much speed, he and the leader jumped clear.

The truck had been left in neutral, and it began to roll faster, spurred ahead by the weight of a fully loaded trailer. From his passenger-side seat, Frank had a bird's-eye view of the steep hills and the rocky gorge that bordered the road. He fell against the door as the rig took a curve.

He thought to himself, I could really enjoy this scenery—if we weren't riding through it in a runaway eighteen-wheeler—with no brakes!

Chapter

12

PAT, SHACKLED TO the wheel, put the rig in gear and tried to control the huge, heavy machine to keep them from flying into the gorge on their left. Despite her best efforts, the truck continued to build up speed.

Frank strained at the door handle to which his handcuff was attached, but the handle held firm. He grabbed the chain with both hands and yanked, but he only succeeded in scraping some skin off his wrist. The door handle didn't give an inch.

"How are you doing?" he yelled to Pat over the noise of the engine.

She was staring grimly straight ahead. It was obvious that she was using all her strength and concentration, fighting to control the steering wheel and to keep the truck's speed down as much as she could with the transmission.

"The trouble is the trailer!" she shouted back. "All that weight—either it's going to push us off the road, or it'll fishtail and drop and pull us down after it."

"Can you unhitch the trailer?" Joe called from the sleeping compartment.

"Not from inside," she replied. "There's a hand-operated backup system, a crank that you turn to retract the kingpin from the fifth wheel, but—"

"Where is it?" Frank asked.

"Behind the cab, just below the frame that holds the fifth wheel in place."

"Could I get to it from here?"

"From here? You mean while we're moving?" Her eyes widened, and she shook her head. "Frank, that's crazy! It'd be suicide to try something like that!"

"It'd be suicide not to do anything at all!" Tony yelled. "When this truck goes over the edge, you *know* that's going to be bad for our health!"

"I'm going for it," Frank called out. He opened the door. "At least this cuff ought to keep me from falling under the wheels!"

As he swung his body out, the wind hit him in the face with powerful force. Close behind him was the steep rise of the hill. Trees and brush jutted out close to his body. A tree branch whipped across his back as he pressed his stomach flat against the body of the tractor. He hung on tight, feeling the harsh rumble and bumping of the huge vehicle, and made himself take slow, deep breaths to stay calm.

With his left foot Frank groped for the first foothold on the side of the cab. He gripped the door frame and lowered himself cautiously, while stretching to get a look behind and beneath, where tractor and trailer joined.

"I see a handle sticking out down there," he shouted, trying to make himself heard over the engine and the rushing wind. "That must be it."

His right hand was anchored to the door handle by the handcuffs, but he reached his left hand back, extending himself as far as possible. He missed the crank by a couple of feet. It was obvious that he couldn't possibly reach it that way.

The truck hurtled around a sharp turn, and Frank's door flew wide open. For a moment he dangled just above the onrushing asphalt road. Grabbing frantically for the door frame with his left hand, he pulled himself back against the side of the cab.

"I'll never get to it this way," he gasped. "Unless—wait a second . . ."

"I can't hold us on the road much longer!" screamed Pat.

Again Frank stretched himself out as far as he could, but this time, instead of reaching with his arm, he extended his left leg as far as it would go. His foot hit the crank handle! He gave it a push, but the handle wouldn't budge. He shoved harder, trying to get all his weight behind it. Branches flew by, some hitting him. Finally, he kicked at the stubborn handle in frustration.

The crank turned! It moved an inch, and then, with Frank's next desperate lunge, it moved farther. When he had pushed it as far as his foot would reach, he hooked his toe around the crank near the pivot and pulled it around toward him again. Alternately pushing and pulling on the handle, he turned the crank around three times. It seemed to take forever, and his body was aching with the strain.

All of a sudden there was a bump, and a slight gap appeared between the tractor and trailer. They were unhitched! Frank hauled himself back up and into the seat.

"Got it!" he cried triumphantly. "We're clear!"

Pat gave the tractor a little gas, and a space widened between the two parts of the rig. As they swung around the next turn, Pat and Frank looked back just in time to see the trailer hurtle wildly off the road and crash down into the trees and bushes of the gully below.

Frank craned his neck around to watch the trailer fall as Pat, free from the trailer's weight, was now able to shift down into the lowest gears and slow the tractor.

"Frank! Brace yourself!" called Pat.

He spun back around to face front, cushioning himself with his knees and free hand as the tractor bumped to a stop against an earth embankment. There was no serious damage to either vehicle or the four imprisoned passengers.

For a moment they all sat, silent.

"Oh, boy!" Tony whispered faintly.

"You're some kind of driver," Joe told Pat.

Pat pointed to the windshield, to where, not a hundred yards ahead of them, the road went into a hairpin turn.

"We would've gone over, right there," she said. "No way could I have made that turn."

No one had anything to say. Each of them just stared at the turn, until Pat spoke again.

"Frank, just behind your seat, there's a toolbox with a hacksaw in it. Let's see if we can't cut loose from all this hardware. Then we'd better head back to Bayport and get someone out here to deal with this rig."

An hour later they had freed themselves from the cab and made their way back uphill to where they had been ambushed. The van still sat in the bushes, and before long they were headed back to Bayport.

"Okay," said Joe from the driver's seat. "Who could have tipped that bunch off that we were coming?"

"How about Hal Brady?" suggested Frank.

"Brady? He wasn't even around, was he?" Tony asked.

"Sure he was," Frank answered. "Remember, Joe? He and Gerard came into Matt's office just when Matt was telling us about this special order for Ultratech. Who knows how long they were hanging out by the door, just listening?"

"And another thing," Joe added. He quickly explained to Tony that Gerard's right-hand man, Turk, was probably the short, stocky thug in the gang. "Brady didn't have to waste much time letting the gang know what was going on."

"Could the whole special order have been a setup?" Frank wondered. "Something that was organized just to get us to a place where we could be trapped?"

"No way," Pat said. "There's too much paperwork involved. Unless there were Ultratech people in on it, too, and that's hard to believe."

"The thing is," Joe said, "that gang wasn't interested in the electronic gear on the truck. They were willing to destroy it, just so long as Lombard wasn't able to make a shipment. Those guys aren't thieves—their job is to put Lombard Hauling out of business."

"Right," said Frank. "And that's why I don't think Lou Gerard is part of the plot. I mean, he may have an argument with Matt, but he wants his people to stay employed."

Pat nodded. "If he's honest, he does."

"Pat, do you think Hal Brady could be the

one passing inside information to this gang?'' asked Frank.

They drove in silence while Pat thought about the question. At length, she spoke.

"I don't know. He's kind of wild. I could see Hal getting caught up with a bunch of thieves, maybe. But this crowd is worse than thieves—they wanted us dead back there, just now. I don't think Hal's *that* bad.''

"Maybe he didn't realize how rough they'd play when he hooked up with them,'' Joe suggested.

"You're certain there's somebody who works at Lombard who's crooked?'' Tony asked. He clearly wasn't happy with that idea.

Frank turned to him and said, "Look at the facts, Tony. You can't get away from it. Nobody knew about today's shipment for Ultratech until this morning. And yet that gang knew not only that it was going out, but what route we'd take and also when we'd get to that spot.

"Even allowing for their being prepared, with stolen trucks and traffic barriers, the hijackers had to have known not very long after Matt found out himself. It had to be someone who was able to get information right at the source.''

Tony looked glum. "Uncle Matt's really going to hate that. He's always said that he feels everybody who works for him is like family.''

"He didn't exactly feel brotherly toward Hal Brady,'' Joe reminded him.

"Oh, that was just a temper thing," Tony insisted. "Matt blows up easy, but he cools down easy, too. I bet he'd have had Hal working again even without that union guy coming in."

"Tony's probably right," agreed Pat. "Matt can sound tough, and goodness knows he can be stubborn, but he doesn't hold grudges."

"Pat, do you know why there's been bad feelings between Matt and Brady lately?" Frank asked. "Felix Kinney says Matt wouldn't tell him, but you're his sister-in-law."

She shook her head. "Sorry, Frank. I can't help you there. Seems like a while back, Hal suddenly got real feisty with Matt, started giving him a lot of lip. But I never heard why."

"Well, we'll be back at Lombard in a few minutes," said Joe. "Then we're going to have a talk with Matt and get a few things straight, I hope."

"And I have to get my rig hauled in for repairs," Pat added. "And check to see how much damage was done to the shipment."

They arrived at Lombard and pulled into the parking area. Two patrol cars from the sheriff's office were parked nearby.

"I wonder what's going on?" Tony said.

"Let's find out," Joe said, getting out of the van.

As they walked toward the office, the door to Matt's office opened. Teri Yarnell walked out, crying. Seeing the approaching group, she ran up to Joe and grabbed his hand.

"Oh, I'm so glad you're back, it's terrible, terrible! You've got to do something."

"Teri, slow down, take it easy," Joe urged gently. "What is it? What's happened?"

More people came out of the office. Felix Kinney appeared, looking shaken, followed by a sheriff's deputy.

Behind the deputy came Matt Simone, a look of helpless anger on his face.

Directly behind Matt, his hand gripping Matt's shoulder and a hard expression on his face, came Chief Deputy Lamar MacReedy.

Chapter

13

JOE STARED AT TERI, then at the group coming out of the office, and then finally at Frank. What was going on? MacReedy seemed pleased with himself, but Matt Simone's jaw muscles were clenched tight with anger.

When he caught sight of the Hardys, Tony, and Pat, MacReedy stopped short and stared. "Where'd *you* come from?"

"What is this?" Tony demanded, running up to his uncle. He whirled around to MacReedy. "Where are you taking him? What's going on here?"

"Tony, take it easy," urged Joe.

"That's good advice," MacReedy said, sounding pompous and smug. "You don't want to interfere with a law officer doing his duty, or you'll find yourself in hot water, just like he is."

Tony appeared ready to explode. Frank reached out to grab his arm, but Tony angrily shook him off.

"Tony!" Matt said sharply. "Don't do anything stupid! You'll just make a bad situation worse."

His words did what Frank and Joe hadn't been able to accomplish. They settled Tony down.

"All right, Deputy," Frank said. "Where are you taking Mr. Simone, and why? Is he under arrest?"

"Not yet. He's going in for questioning, not that it's any of your business." MacReedy gestured to the other officer, who took Matt's arm and led him toward one of the patrol cars.

As he walked, Matt turned to the group and said, with a bitter smile on his face, "He thinks I'm trying to destroy my own company, that I'm working with a gang of thieves and killers! He thinks *I* had something to do with the murder of that guy Vane! Tony, call Mike and have him get my lawyer. This is crazy!" He uttered his last words as the officer helped him into the backseat of the cruiser.

"Okay, Uncle Matt! Don't worry!"

"Be calm, Matt!" called Joe as MacReedy opened the driver's door of the other cruiser. "He's got no grounds to charge you with anything! He's just blowing smoke!"

MacReedy froze with his hand on the door and glared at Joe. "Just like your old man," he muttered angrily. Then he slid into the car.

"That's a compliment, MacReedy!" shouted Joe as the two cars began to roll.

Tony ran inside to call Mike. Frank and Joe stayed in the parking lot with Pat and Felix and Teri.

"Can you guys handle this?" Pat asked. "I've got a rig to tow in."

Frank nodded as she left. Then he turned to Felix. "Any idea why MacReedy took Matt in?"

Felix was staring off into space and didn't seem to have heard the question. He was pale, and he nervously ran a hand through his sandy hair. Abruptly he stopped and turned to Frank. "Sorry, did you ask me something?" Felix asked.

"Did you hear any of what MacReedy said to Matt? Why he suspects him?"

"He—they searched this Mickey Vane's apartment and found notes in Matt's handwriting, giving times and routes of Ultratech shipments, including the ones that were hijacked. There was also a check from a Lombard account made out to Vane.

"Deputy MacReedy says Matt was plotting with Mickey Vane to destroy Lombard Hauling and then collect the insurance. He thinks Matt and Vane were splitting the money from the sale of stolen Ultratech products. He all but accused Matt of having Vane killed to keep him quiet."

"That doesn't make any sense at all," said Joe.

Felix went on. "Deputy MacReedy says that Lombard was in trouble anyway, money trouble and union trouble, and that Matt panicked and was trying to salvage what he could from a bad situation."

Tony came out of the building and joined them. "Mike is calling Matt's lawyer, and they're both going down to the sheriff's office right away. I'm going over there, too." He looked at Frank and Joe. "You guys coming?"

"We'll follow you," Frank assured him. "This is all going to be straightened out, Tony. MacReedy is way off base, and we're going to prove it."

Tony grinned at the Hardys. "I know you're in our corner, and I appreciate it. Now—let's get going!"

At the sheriff's office, they met Matt's lawyer and Mike Simone. The boys were glad to see that Mike, who'd gotten out of the hospital the day before, looked a little better. There weren't so many bandages, and some of the swelling had gone down. He hugged Tony with his good arm.

The lawyer was introduced as James Willis, a gray-haired man in a three-piece suit and gold-rimmed glasses. At Frank's request, he agreed to arrange a meeting for them with Matt while he and Mike worked to "clear up this unfortunate misunderstanding," as he put it.

Willis was true to his word. Within fifteen minutes Frank, Joe, and Tony were sitting with Matt in an unused office. Quickly they filled Matt in on the latest hijacking attempt and the narrow escape they'd had.

"You said you'd tell us what we needed to know as soon as we got back from this trip," Joe said. "Well, we're back."

"Fair enough," Matt replied. "I agreed to answer your questions. So, ask away. I won't hold anything back this time."

"Start with Lou Gerard," Frank suggested.

"I always got along fine with the union people," Matt said, "until Gerard showed up in my office. He told me he was the local's new business manager. We made some small talk, and then all of a sudden he tells me that contract negotiations and grievance procedures would go a lot easier for me if I was to slip him some cash under the table now and then.

"I lost my temper and kicked him out. But he started calling me up, demanding to meet with me and making threats about the future of my company if I didn't play ball. 'You have to go along to get along,' he said. ''I said, 'No way.' ''

"You have any proof of this?" asked Frank.

Matt shook his head. "He was too smart. He never talked about it unless he was sure there was nobody around, and he arranged our meetings in places where I couldn't tape our conversations."

"Why not bring in the law?" Frank demanded.

"With no proof?" Matt leaned forward. "Lombard Hauling is a small operation, Frank. We do all right, but we can't afford to shut down for long. So what happens if I blow the whistle on Gerard?"

Matt leaned forward, speaking emphatically. "First off, he tells the law that *I* was the one offering *him* bribes in exchange for special favors. His word against mine, right? Then he has the power to call everyone off the job. But I have to keep the business going, and it doesn't matter whether I was right or wrong, the result is the same—we'd be shut down. So I didn't holler for the cops or the sheriff."

"Maybe you should have," Joe suggested.

"Well, maybe. But that was my choice. And once I made that choice, I had to play it out. That's the way I saw it—and still see it."

"All right," said Joe. "Number two—what problem does Hal Brady have with you?"

Matt shrugged. "You got me. I don't know."

Frank leaned toward him. "Hey, you promised to level with us."

"I am," Matt protested. "Brady and I were never buddies, but we didn't have any beefs, either. Then all of a sudden, a few months back, he just took a dislike to me, started giving me a lot of lip and griping about this and that—generally getting on my case. Well, I admit I have a temper, and I lost it sometimes. But *why* it all started, I don't know. You'd better ask him.''

"Did you get to see the notes that were found in Mickey's Vane's apartment?" Joe asked.

"They showed them to me, yeah."

"Did you recognize them?"

"Recognize them?" Matt shook his head. "I recognized them as being my handwriting, sure. I'm always making notes on scratch paper like that. I don't know when or how I made those particular ones. But I can tell you one thing. I never gave them to Mickey Vane."

Joe nodded, then asked, "Any explanation for how they got to be where they were found? And that Lombard company check, you signed that, too, didn't you?"

"*I* never gave them to him. I never *saw* the man after I canned him a couple years ago. It wouldn't have been hard to steal blank checks from my desk. Vane got no checks I knew about after he drew his last pay."

"Matt," said Joe, "do you think that Hal Brady could be the one responsible for passing information to the gang?"

Matt thought for a moment. "He could be," he said, "if he knows anything about computers. We store everything on computers now, so he'd have to know how to retrieve the information."

Everyone turned as James Willis entered the room and sat down. "We'll have you out of here soon," he told Matt. "That chief deputy is giving us some grief, but I've told him that if he isn't charging you, he can't hold you. And he hasn't got anything solid enough, just a lot of circumstantial nonsense."

"Great." Matt managed a tired smile. He turned to Frank and Joe. "Anything else you need to know?"

"I don't think so," Joe said. "Anything we can do for you?"

"Well, yes, if you don't mind. If Felix is still at the office, tell him everything is going to be fine and have him call up my insurance man. If he's gone home for the night, then you call him. You can get his name and number off my desk. Here, take my office keys." He handed them to Joe.

"Sure, no problem," Frank said. "Tony, want to come?"

"No, that's okay," Tony said. "I'm going to drive Mike home. See you guys later."

Joe and Frank shook hands with Matt and left. As they were driving the van back to Lombard, Frank said, "Maybe Dad has turned up something on Brady. He had the opportunity to leak information, and for whatever reason, it looks like he's mad enough at Matt to want to get at him."

"If he can operate a computer, then he had the means of doing it, too," Joe added. "Motive, means, opportunity. If Hal checks out in all three, we've got ourselves a prime suspect."

When they arrived at the Lombard office, it appeared to be dark and deserted. "Felix must have called it a night," Frank said.

"I can't blame him," Joe replied, stifling a yawn. "It's late. We're putting in some crazy hours, too."

As they got out of the van, Joe noticed someone standing in the shadows near the office door.

"Who's there?" he called.

At first the figure didn't move, and Joe wondered if they were in for another fight. As he and Frank approached, the other person moved out into the open. It was Hal Brady, and he didn't look happy to see them.

"What're *you* doing here?" Brady growled.

"We could ask you the same question," said Frank. "We're here to do something for Matt Simone."

Brady snorted. "Something for Simone, huh? Beautiful. Well, I'm here to do something *about* Matt Simone."

"What are you talking about?" Frank asked.

"We're going to show Simone up for the rotten thief and liar he is," Brady said, his voice harsh with anger.

"You're not making sense, Brady," Joe said.

"No?" Brady stepped to within a foot of Joe and snarled, "Wait till we get those papers out of his desk! You'll see what a bum he is!"

"You said 'we,' Brady. You and who else?"

"Lou Gerard," Brady replied. "He told me to

meet him here. Says there are papers in Simone's desk that'll prove how he's been cheating his employees, not paying into the pension fund, not keeping up with the health and welfare payments, just squeezing the company dry until he can take the money and run.''

"Lou Gerard told you this?" asked Frank.

"That's right," Brady said. "And he asked me to help him nail Simone."

A car drove up to the Lombard gate and stopped, its engine still running. A voice called out, "Brady? Is that you?"

"Yeah, it's me," Brady answered. "Lou?"

One of the car windows rolled down. Brady took a step closer.

Frank saw movement in the dark car. There was a brief glint of light as something metallic was raised to the open window.

"Brady, get down!" Frank yelled.

Shots rang out in the quiet lot!

Chapter

14

FRANK LEAPED AT the astonished Hal Brady and bulldogged him to the ground. A bullet that would have caught the big driver squarely in the chest ripped through the sleeve of his shirt instead, just grazing the skin. The other shots passed harmlessly overhead.

From his position flat on the pavement, Frank heard the car doors open and then slam. Three men got out. Three flashlights snapped on and began to cut through the darkness, searching out their target—and anyone else who got in the way. Each man held a flashlight and an automatic pistol.

"Frank! Brady!" Joe's whisper came from behind a large metal trash container on wheels near the wall. "Over here!"

Frank tapped Hal Brady's shoulder. "Stay with me! Stay low and keep quiet!"

He crawled toward the protection of the trash bin, with Brady just behind him. They ducked between the bin and the wall, where they found Joe crouched.

"What—" Brady started to say, but at a furious gesture from Joe, he lowered his voice to a whisper. "Who *are* those guys? I don't understand!"

"It's your buddy Lou Gerard, or some of his friends," Joe said softly. "He's the one who got you to come here, isn't he?"

"Yeah, but—"

"He set you up, Brady!" Frank hissed. He carefully peered out from behind their cover, then ducked back. "One of them's headed straight for us."

"But—but *why!*" Brady was stunned. His eyes were wide, and he was shaking his head, trying to make sense of the mystery.

"Later for that," Joe said. "Right now, staying alive is our top priority."

The three gunmen had fanned out, and Frank saw that one was approaching the Dumpster.

"On my signal," Frank whispered to the others, "shove this thing forward, hard. Then we'll try to wheel it toward the office and use it as a shield until we get inside."

"Hey!" came the voice of the closest thug, only a few feet from the bin now. "I think I hear 'em!"

"Go!" Frank snapped, not bothering to keep his voice down. He, Joe, and Brady pushed the big trash container forward, ramming it into the gunman. The man fell, and it sounded as if his flashlight broke as he went down.

Joe darted out to get the bulky bin moving in the right direction, then ducked back behind it as shots rang out from two guns. He heard the shots bounce off the metal, as the bin creaked toward the door to the offices.

The goons stalked them as Frank twisted the key in the lock and swung the door open. He and Brady dived in first, followed by Joe, who dragged the bin across the doorway, where their pursuers would use up a few seconds getting it out of the way. Brady grabbed an ignition key off a rack in the office. The group dashed for the garage, which stood dark and shut down for the night.

Once in the garage, they stopped to listen. They could hear the Dumpster being moved from the door, and then they heard footsteps in Matt's office. Joe risked a quick look back and said quietly, "There are two of them in there. They must've left one on guard outside."

The attack had taken Brady by surprise, but he caught on fast. "This is the key to my old rig. The tractor's three down, with the custom chrome work on the sides. If one of you can open the garage door to the outside, we might be able to break out of here."

The door was raised by a chain and pulley

system, Brady explained. "I'll do it," said Joe. "How's the arm, Brady? Are you all right?"

Startled, Brady noticed for the first time a dark stain on the right sleeve of his shirt. "It's nothing, just a graze," he said. "I didn't even know I was hit."

Frank stationed himself next to the door that led to the offices, pressing himself flat against the wall. Joe went to the outside garage door and grasped the chain to raise it as Hal Brady quickly clambered up into the cab of his old semi.

When Joe gave him a high sign, Brady started the truck's powerful diesel engine. Then Joe pulled the chain, arm over arm, raising the corrugated metal door with a loud rattle.

A bright beam lit up Joe as a gunman holding a flashlight came through the entryway from the office. He had his gun leveled at Joe, ready to shoot, as Frank chopped at the man's wrist with the edge of his right hand. The gun clattered to the concrete. The man turned in surprise and was hit flush on the jaw by Frank's left hook. The man fell, landing on top of his gun.

The garage door rattled up, revealing a second gunman—one had been left outside. He, too, was poised to shoot as Hal started the truck forward and turned on his blinding headlights and leaned on the truck's deafening klaxon horn. The hood, who was standing directly in front of the oncoming machine, was forced to dive off to the side.

Frank bent to move the man he had dropped to get his pistol, but he was knocked aside by a sudden impact. The third hood had slammed into him! Tucking into a shoulder roll, Frank somersaulted and sprang back to his feet. He was caught now between the gunman who had knocked him down and the first one, who was getting up. Joe was screened from the action by the truck, Frank realized, so he wouldn't know to come help.

With his airhorn still blasting the night silence, Brady gunned his engine and drove forward, smashing the gangsters' car broadside where it stood in the entrance to the Lombard lot. He shifted into reverse, and it looked as if he was going to ram the car again.

The guy outside, a tall, brawny type, yelled, "He's going to wreck the car! Let's beat it before we can't get out of here."

The three men made it to the car before Brady maneuvered back for a second attack. They took off, the car wobbling from the damage done to the chassis by the heavy truck.

Hal Brady climbed down from the cab. "Should we go after them?"

"No," Frank said. "They've still got guns."

Brady frowned and rubbed his chin thoughtfully. "That big, burly one—I've seen him somewhere, I'm sure of it."

"We have, too," Joe said quietly to his brother. "Only tonight he wasn't wearing a mask."

"They must have figured they wouldn't be leaving any witnesses," said Frank. Turning to Brady, he asked, "Can you remember where you saw him?"

After a few seconds the trucker sighed. "I'm drawing a blank, but it'll come to me." Then he stared at the Hardys with new interest.

"What gives here? Those guys wanted to kill me! And what's the story with you two? Don't tell me you're just a couple of kids who work for Simone—kids don't handle themselves like you did when they're up against professional muscle. Talk to me!"

Frank considered the situation a moment. "Okay, Brady," he said. "Just do this for us—go in the office and punch up the week's trip schedule on the computer. And we'll tell you what's going on."

"Punch up?" Brady sputtered. "What I know about computers you could write on a matchbook cover."

Again, Frank looked at Joe, who was grinning.

"Brady, you just passed the test," Joe said. "Let's talk. The only one who knew you'd be here tonight was Gerard, right?"

"But why would Gerard want me dead?"

"We don't know yet," Frank answered. "You probably know something that you shouldn't, something that could help put Gerard away."

Brady was looking at them as if they were

crazy. "But I don't—put *Gerard* away? But it's *Simone* who—"

"Did Gerard tell you something about Matt being a crook a while back?"

"He told me that Simone was bleeding money out of the company, that he was messing around with the books. And that soon he'd take all this money and let the business go under and retire to some place in the sun, where they could never bring him back to face the music."

"Brady," Frank interrupted. "Gerard is bent. He's been trying to extort money from Matt, in exchange for going real easy on contract talks and so on. But Matt wasn't going along, so Gerard decided to up the pressure."

"You mean—" Light dawned in Hal Brady's eyes. "Like this hijacking business?"

"Right," Joe said. "Gerard has this driver called Turk—looks and talks like an old boxer who's been hit too often. We're pretty sure he's one of the hijackers. And these three tonight are probably the others."

Brady suddenly smacked a fist into his other hand. "I *knew* I'd seen that big guy before! I had a meeting with Gerard a week ago, and when I arrived, that guy was there. He left right after I arrived."

"That's probably why Gerard wanted you out of the way," said Joe. "Because you could tie him to the hijackers. And now *we'll* be on the hit list, too," he added.

"Sure," Frank agreed. "He probably hoped that when your body was found, Deputy MacReedy might guess that Matt had had it done. Everyone knew there was bad feeling between you."

Hal Brady looked angry, then embarrassed. "Then I've been a fool, treating Matt Simone like a criminal."

"Matt'll understand, once you explain that Gerard suckered you," said Joe.

"Suckered me!" Brady looked angry again. "He almost *killed* me! I want to get face-to-face with that little creep. Right now!"

"Slow down, Brady!" Frank warned. "First we have to get proof." He turned to Joe. "Let's check in with Dad."

They called Fenton from Matt's phone.

"Sorry," came Fenton's voice from the other end of the line. "That tow truck was reported stolen last week, just as you suspected. And I couldn't find anything on this Hal Brady. He seems to be clean."

"That's okay, Dad," Frank replied. He motioned to another phone on a small table in a corner, and Joe listened in. "We already worked that one out for ourselves. But didn't you say something about Mickey Vane being suspected of involvement with labor racketeering?"

"Vane? That's right."

"Did you get anything more in that area?" They could hear Fenton going through some papers.

"Here it is. Vane was mixed up with a man named Leonard Garry, who was wanted in California in connection with some missing union funds. Garry is still at large. Does that help any?"

"It sure does," Frank replied. "Thanks, Dad. See you later."

"What are the odds that Lou Gerard is Leonard Garry?" he asked Joe after they'd hung up.

"No bet," Joe answered. "If we could get Gerard's fingerprints and match them with Garry's, that'd pretty much be the ball game."

Brady's expression brightened. "There ought to be stuff with Gerard's prints in his office at the local," he said. "Let's get over there!"

Frank checked his watch. "It's pretty late, Hal. How do we get in?"

Brady pulled a key ring from his pocket and flipped through it until he found the one he wanted. "I was a shop steward there for a while, and they gave me this so I could get into the office if I needed to. If no one's around, so much the better. We can roust Gerard's office in private. Let me just put my rig back in the garage, and then we can get going."

But when they arrived at the union's local office in the Hardys' van, they were surprised to find lights on.

"Looks like Gerard is working late tonight," Brady said, disappointed.

They were parked across the street. "Let's

hang out here a little," suggested Joe. "Maybe he'll knock off soon, and we can look around."

Half an hour went by before the lights in Gerard's office went out and the front door opened.

"Here we go," Joe murmured.

They watched as Lou Gerard appeared on the sidewalk, but he wasn't alone. He spoke briefly with another man before getting into a car and driving off. Joe couldn't quite make out the other man's features, since he was standing on an unlit part of the sidewalk.

The man stood there, nervously tapping his foot before he walked to his own car, which was parked under a streetlight. As he unlocked and opened the door, he glanced back over his shoulder, and his face was clearly lit from the lamp above. Joe sucked in his breath sharply.

There was no mistaking the face of Felix Kinney.

Chapter

15

"THERE'S OUR INFORMANT," Frank said quietly.

Hal Brady was stunned. "Felix? I can't believe it! He's been with Simone for fifteen years! He's a nice guy, wouldn't hurt a fly."

"Maybe, but he's also a logical suspect," pointed out Joe. "Think about it. He has total access to the computer, he knows everything about Lombard's shipments, when and where they go and what's on them. And, come to think of it, Teri said he's been putting in a lot of late hours recently, even though business has been slow."

Felix had started his car by then, and pulled away from the curb.

"Let's tail him," Frank said. "Gerard's fingerprints will keep until tomorrow."

Starting up the van, Frank made a U-turn to follow Kinney.

"Don't get too close," warned Joe. "Traffic is light, and we don't want him to spot us."

"Thanks for the hot tip, super sleuth," Frank said sarcastically.

But Felix appeared not to notice them, and before long it was clear where they were headed.

"He's going to Lombard," Frank observed as they made a left turn onto the road that led down to the trucking company.

A few minutes later Felix parked in front of the Lombard building and let himself in. Frank had dropped well back as soon as Felix's destination was obvious. He stopped the van at the corner of the block, where they weren't too close but could keep an eye on the building.

"We'll give him a couple of minutes and then go in to find out what he's up to," Frank said.

They waited in silence. A dim light went on in Felix's office. Another minute went by.

"Let's go," Joe said.

They were quiet, not wanting to warn Felix of their presence. Frank used Matt's key to unlock the front door, and the three of them crept to the door to Felix's office, which stood ajar.

Frank saw Felix sitting with his back to them, hunched over a computer console. As he worked the keys, figures flashed in neon green on the screen. He looked at a sheet of paper and scrawled notes on it from time to time, copying data from the display.

"Hi, Felix," Frank said, stepping into the room.

Kinney let out a startled noise and stood up, spinning around to face them.

"Working kind of late tonight, aren't you?" asked Joe, as he and Brady came in behind Frank.

"Oh, hi. You gave me a scare there for a second." Felix tried to smile but couldn't hold it and had to shift his eyes away. "Yeah, I was, uh—I forgot to enter some stuff on the computer so I thought I'd . . ." His voice trailed off and there was a brief silence.

"You're keeping some bad company, too, aren't you?" said Joe.

Felix backed up a step. "What do you mean by that?" He sounded shrill, and he wouldn't meet Joe's gaze. "I had *work* to do, I told you!"

"Work for who? Not for Lombard, I'll bet." Frank advanced very close to the edgy accountant. Felix backed up.

"Listen here, I don't know what you're talking about." Felix had an annoyed look on his face, but it couldn't mask his fear. "And it's not a good time for bad jokes, so just—go home and—"

"It's no good, Kinney," Frank said. "We saw you with Lou Gerard tonight at his office, and we followed you here. We know all about him— and you, too."

Hal Brady couldn't keep quiet any longer.

"*Why*, Felix? Why did you do it? Gerard fed me a line of garbage and I bought it, but *you*—Simone treated you good! I just don't get it."

Suddenly Felix's knees gave way, and he collapsed into his desk chair, burying his face in his hands.

Frank squatted down beside him. "Felix?" He spoke gently, softly. "The game is up. We're taking everything we know to the sheriff. The best thing you can do for yourself is tell us what you know, and maybe that'll make things a little better for you. We can say you cooperated with us, at the end."

Felix raised his head and drew in a ragged breath. His face was pasty white. "What I did—I didn't have any choice. I *had* to!"

"Tell us," Frank urged.

"A couple of years ago I ran into heavy expenses and I didn't have the money to meet them. I panicked. I know, I know," Felix said, "I should have gone to Matt and he'd have given me what I needed. Well, I wasn't thinking, I was scared. I took some money from Lombard's expense account and fiddled with the computer to hide it for a while."

Felix took another deep breath before continuing. "I told myself, 'It's just a loan, I'll pay it back and no one will ever know.' But time went by and I couldn't get it together, and I *knew* I'd be found out. I wound up going to a—someone I heard about, who'd give me what I needed."

"A loan shark?" Frank asked. "Felix, guys like that will lend you money, no questions asked, but will bleed you dry afterward."

Felix nodded. "That's what I discovered. I kept paying and paying, and the debt never got any smaller. Then one day, after I'd been paying this guy for months, he said he'd sold my debt to another man and that I'd deal with him from now on. And that man turned out to be—"

"Lou Gerard," Joe finished for him.

"Exactly," Felix said grimly. "Gerard came and said he wasn't interested in getting money from me. What he wanted was 'little favors' —that's what he called them. Information on Lombard, routes and schedules and cargo. And then he wanted other things—stuff off Matt's desk, in his handwriting, and some blank Lombard company checks—"

"Which wound up in Mickey Vane's apartment," Joe said.

"When they came to take Matt in for questioning," Felix went on, "and I heard what the evidence was against him, things that *I* had supplied, I almost blurted out the truth right then and there. But—I couldn't. Just didn't have the guts, I guess."

"Are you willing to tell the sheriff everything you've told us?" Frank asked.

"If I do, will I still have to go to jail?"

Frank leaned closer over Felix's chair. "Felix, I'm not going to lie to you," he said in a quiet voice. "You committed a felony, and that's probably going to mean a prison term. But if you have no previous record and you help us now and agree to testify against Gerard and his gang, they'll take that into account. You won't do as much time as you would otherwise."

"It doesn't matter," Felix said. "I'll do whatever you want. I owe Matt that much, anyway."

"That's the truth," muttered Brady. He had been glaring at Felix all during the painful confession.

"Lighten up, Brady," Joe cautioned. "Remember, you gave Matt some grief, too."

Brady flushed. "Yeah, you're right. Sorry, Kinney. So, what now? We call the sheriff and dump this in his lap and he grabs Gerard, huh?"

"That's one way to go," said Frank. "But there are a couple of things I don't like about it."

"Such as?" asked Joe.

"First, some of those hoods who tried to kill us might get away if they aren't all tied up in a neat bundle. And second," Frank said, grinning at Joe, "we're missing a chance to rub MacReedy's nose in it by handing him the whole thing on a platter. I mean, how sore is he going to be when *we* give him his collar?"

Joe grinned back. "He'd have to smile and say 'Thank you.' Beautiful! How do we set it up?"

"With Felix's help," Frank said, looking at the bookkeeper. "If he's willing."

"I'm willing," Felix said. "What can I do?"

"You can tip Gerard off that a really major shipment of Ultratech products is going out of here tomorrow. Can you arrange that?"

"Sure!" Felix had lost his hangdog look, and now seemed eager to help. "I could fake a cargo manifest and route it anywhere you want."

"Then what?" asked Brady.

"We send out a truck as bait," Frank explained, "and pick a route with a likely spot for an ambush. Pat drives the truck, like on the other hauls, and we follow it—Tony, Joe, me—"

"Count me in on this one," growled Brady. "I want a piece of Gerard myself."

"The more the better," Frank told him. "Anyway, tomorrow morning, we call MacReedy and tell him to arrest Gerard at his office and then meet us where the ambush is likely to happen, with a load of deputies and a net. That way we get the whole bunch, and MacReedy has to thank us and apologize to Matt."

"That last part is my favorite," said Joe. "I might want to get that on videotape."

Felix sat down at his computer console. "I'll put that phony cargo manifest together now."

"Great!" Joe turned to Hal Brady. "You have an idea about the route? It should be mostly heavily traveled roads, except for one stretch that's a hijacker's dream. We want to pinpoint where they'll grab us as close as we can."

The trucker thought a bit, then smiled. "I got

just the route for the job. I drive it a lot, and it's perfect. Mostly superhighway, except for five miles of local roads, made to order for a thief.''

"Fantastic!" exclaimed Frank. "Felix can print it out for Gerard when he's finished with the manifest.''

"This manifest won't take me long," said Felix. He bent over his console and began working the keyboard. "I'm putting enough audio equipment in this shipment to make Gerard's mouth water.''

Frank sat on a corner of the desk, watching Kinney work and admiring his expert handling of the computer. Joe paced back and forth in the little room, and Hal Brady lounged by the window, staring out at the deserted street.

Suddenly Brady stiffened. Leaning forward, he pressed closer to the window. "Hey! We got trouble!" he whispered.

Frank, Joe, and Felix all stopped what they were doing.

"What's up?" Frank asked, standing quickly and going over to Brady.

Brady jerked a thumb out the window. "It's that bruiser of Gerard's—Turk. He just parked a car outside, and he's headed this way!"

Chapter

16

FRANK GLANCED QUICKLY out the window. The
short, muscular hood was walking across the
parking area! Felix jumped up nervously. "What's
he doing here now?" he asked.

"We can't let him see us here!" snapped Joe.
"Let's wait in the next office. You, too, Brady!
Felix, just act natural."

"But—"

"Remember, Turk thinks you're on *his* side.
As long as he thinks that, everything will be
fine," said Frank.

Felix still looked shaky.

"Turk isn't exactly a brain surgeon," Joe told
the accountant, pausing in the doorway. "String
him along. You can do it, Felix. We're counting
on you."

Felix licked his lips and nodded. The other three slipped into the next office and quietly closed the connecting door.

In the dark room, Hal Brady muttered, "I sure hope he doesn't blow it."

"*Sssh!*" Frank hissed. A second later they heard Felix speak.

"Turk! What brings you down here this late?"

"Mr. Gerard wants some stationery with Lombard Hauling printed on it. He got an idea, and he said you'd probably be here."

"Stationery? Sure thing." A desk drawer slid open. "Here you go. Turk, wait a minute!"

"Uh-oh," Brady whispered.

"What is it, Kinney? I gotta get back. Mr. Gerard told me to hurry."

"I have big news for Mr. Gerard, Turk. He'll want to know."

Frank held his breath. What was Felix doing?

"Tell Mr. Gerard that we're sending out a big order from Ultratech tomorrow. I just heard about it. In fact"—there was a sound of paper tearing—"give Mr. Gerard this. It's a copy of the list of goods going out on the truck. Tell him I'll have the exact route the truck is taking later and I'll drop off a copy for him."

"Okay," said Turk, and a door closed.

Several seconds later Felix opened the connecting door. "Come on out. He's gone."

"Why did you tell Turk about the shipment

now?'' Joe demanded, stepping angrily into Felix's office.

"Why not?" asked Felix.

"Because it's the middle of the night, that's why not!" Joe was hot. "That's got to sound fishy."

Felix shook his head. "Not fishy," he said, "just urgent. And that'll make the hijack harder for Gerard to resist."

"All right, Felix," Frank said, giving Joe a look that said "Back off." "You did good work there. Now, let Brady give you that route so you can pass it on. Then we can finally get out of here and—"

The phone rang on Felix's desk. Felix picked it up. "Hello? Yes, Mr. Simone—just a second." He handed the phone to Joe, explaining, 'It's Matt Simone. He and Mike just got home."

"Let's set up a meeting here first thing in the morning to get ourselves organized," Frank suggested.

Joe nodded and spoke into the phone. "Hello, Matt? There's been a lot going on. If you can be here at seven tomorrow morning with Mike, Pat, and Tony, we'll fill you in and tell you what we're setting up. . . . No, it's too complicated to tell you now. . . . Let's just say we hope to wrap the whole thing up by late tomorrow afternoon. . . . Right . . . See you in the morning."

He hung up.

"Seven A.M., huh? I'll be here," said Brady. "Guess I'll apologize to Matt for starters."

Felix sighed. "I'd better be here, too—if Matt will let me on the premises, that is."

"Hang in there, Felix," Frank said. "We *will* need you in the morning, and I'm sure Matt will see that you're trying to make up for what you did."

"Get some sleep, everybody," advised Joe. "I figure we're going to need it."

The following morning at seven-thirty the Hardys, Tony Prito, Matt and Mike Simone, Pat Mulvaney, and Hal Brady stood in a tight group watching Felix Kinney on the telephone.

"That's right, Mr. Gerard," said the bookkeeper. "Yes, sir, I figured you'd want to know about the shipment right away. . . . Yes . . . Thanks . . . I will." He hung up the receiver and looked at the others.

"He said that this should be the last straw for Lombard Hauling, and he told me my debt is now paid in full."

Nobody smiled. Matt, who'd heard the whole story earlier, said, "Well, you've paid a piece of your debt to me, too. Not all of it, Felix, but some."

"Hal, you and Pat and Tony can start loading the truck," Matt went on. "We can use a lot of the Ultratech components that we salvaged from the trailer yesterday."

"If this 'shipment' is just a dummy for bait," said Joe, "how come we're actually loading up the truck? Why not just send it out empty?"

Pat Mulvaney replied, "Because at least a couple of the guys in this gang are experienced with long-haul rigs, Joe. They'd be able to spot an empty truck from the way it rides. We don't want to tip them off, do we?"

As the loading started, Frank noticed that Pat was being extra careful in her checkout procedure. He could see why. She wouldn't be driving her regular tractor, which was being repaired, so it was doubly important to check everything over.

As he helped Pat run through the list, Frank glanced over at Mike, who was leaning against the garage wall near the door to the office, watching the preparations. Mike had wanted to be in on the action, but Frank and Joe had persuaded him that his broken arm would make him a hindrance. He would wait at the office.

When Teri Yarnell arrived shortly before eight o'clock, Joe went over to say hello. She looked surprised to see so much going on.

"Everyone's off to an early start today," she commented.

"There's a lot to get done," Joe said.

Teri's brown eyes went wide when she saw Hal Brady walk by. "What's *he* doing here?" she asked. "I thought he was suspended after that fight with Mr. Simone."

"They worked everything out, and he's back

at work," Joe said. "Listen, Teri, you like movies?"

"Love them," she said, smiling.

"Me, too," said Joe. "Do you eat dinner?"

"Every night."

"What do you know, so do I!" He gave her a big grin, and she giggled. "You want to eat dinner and see a movie together? Like, say, Saturday night?"

"Saturday? I'd love to. Wait a second." She grabbed a piece of notepaper and wrote on it. "Here's my address and phone number. Call me tonight, okay?"

Joe looked up as Matt stuck his head out his office door and called, "Joe! We need you in here a second."

"On my way," Joe answered. Then, turning back to Teri, he said, "At least we finally got to finish our conversation."

Joe was still smiling when he reached Matt's office, where the mood was all business.

"I just want to make certain that everything is set," Matt said. "That truck will be ready to go in fifteen minutes, and I'll be in it with Pat. Tony and Hal will follow in Hal's truck. I've rented a car for you two," he added, gesturing to Frank and Joe, "because the gang knows that van of yours by now and if it's anywhere around, it might make them suspicious. The rental car has a CB unit, so you can keep in touch. Anything I've forgotten?"

"The only thing left to do is call MacReedy," Frank told him.

"Be my guest." Matt handed him the phone.

As Frank was getting the number, Joe asked, "Can I listen in?" Matt gestured to the extension, which Joe picked up.

"Sheriff's Department, Chief Deputy MacReedy," said the familiar hard voice over the line.

"Good morning, Deputy, this is Frank Hardy."

"Hardy? What do you want, boy? I told you to stay out of my hair."

"Sorry to bother you, Deputy. I just thought you'd like to know that we know who's responsible for the hijackings at Lombard Hauling."

"You *what?* Is this some kind of a joke?"

"It's no joke. If you listen for a minute, you can wrap up the whole business today."

There was a short silence on the other end of the line.

"All right," MacReedy said at last. "Say what you have to say."

"Okay. First of all, the man behind the whole scheme is Lou Gerard—"

"Gerard! Now, hold on, there! Where on earth did you get the notion—"

"It's not a notion, Deputy MacReedy. We have proof that'll stand up in any court that Gerard organized it. He was trying to extort payoffs from Matt Simone, but Matt wouldn't pay."

"Is that it? Arrest Lou Gerard?"

"Well, there's a little more, Deputy," Frank said. "We've set a little trap for the rest of the gang. We let Gerard hear about a shipment leaving here in a few minutes, and we're sure he won't be able to resist trying to grab it. We set it up so we know where and when they'll take the truck. So all you have to do is be five miles north of the intersection of Routes Seventy-four and One fifteen with some men at two-thirty this afternoon, and you'll have a nice collar for your record. And you don't even have to give us any credit. How does that grab you?"

There was another thoughtful silence from the deputy's end.

"Okay, Hardy. Maybe you've got something. How big is this gang, and how do you know they'll be where you think they'll be?"

Frank quickly told MacReedy the details and the sheriff's officer said that he'd take care of it.

When Frank hung up, Joe laughed. "I'd love to have seen the look on MacReedy's face when you gave him the word."

Frank nodded, but without much enthusiasm.

"For someone who's just solved a case, you sure don't seem too happy about it," said Joe.

Frank shrugged. "When all the bad guys are locked up and all the good ones are safe, then I'll feel like celebrating. Right now is too soon."

Matt stood up. "Let's get it on the road. I want to see this whole thing behind me, too."

A short while later Pat Mulvaney drove her

eighteen-wheeler out of the yard, with Matt Simone sitting in the shotgun seat. A few minutes afterward Hal Brady got his rig out, too. Tony Prito sat beside him. Then Frank got behind the wheel of the rented car, and Joe joined him. They pulled out behind Hal, bringing up the rear of the parade.

As they drove away, Frank asked, "You think this'll work?"

"It better," Joe replied. "I have a date with Teri for Saturday night, and I plan to show up in one piece."

Two hours later Frank and Joe pulled off the highway and into a huge truck stop. Joe was impressed by the activity as they walked into the busy restaurant. Dozens of tables were filled with truckers who were chowing down, drinking strong coffee, making calls from the telephones placed at each table, exchanging news with buddies, and joking with the waitresses. Looking to the far end of the restaurant, Joe saw there was an area where some gearjammers were renting towels to take showers or catching naps.

He spotted Pat Mulvaney and Matt Simone in one of the booths. Matt gave them a high sign, and he and Frank went over. Pat was just finishing a piece of apple pie, and Matt had a cup of coffee in front of him.

"Everything should be ready to go," Joe told them.

Pat pushed away her plate. "Hal must be in place by now." Hal Brady and Tony were supposed to be parked in a rest stop a few miles farther up the road. It had been decided that it would be better if all three vehicles didn't rendezvous together.

"Okay," said Matt. "The turnoff onto the local road is maybe ten minutes from here. Give us about that long before you get back on the road, and check in with Hal when you do. We'll see you a little later this afternoon."

"That's a ten-four," Joe replied, putting a CB twang in his voice. "Keep the metal side up and the rubber side down, now."

"I sure hope MacReedy's on time," Pat said. She seemed edgy but managed a laugh. "It's kind of funny. Here I am a trucker, and I'm actually looking forward to seeing Smokey. Must be a first."

Joe knew that "Smokey" was trucker's CB lingo for a law officer.

"Let's go, Pat," said Matt. He dropped a couple of bills on the table, gave Frank and Joe a quick thumbs-up sign, and walked out of the restaurant with his sister-in-law.

When the brothers got into their car a few minutes later, Joe picked up the CB mike.

"Mr. P., this is Tailend Charlie. Come in, Mr. P., over."

Tony's voice crackled over the loudspeaker.

"Tailend Charlie, this is Mr. P. We are in position, and ready to move, over."

"When we pass your location, we'll give you a holler," Joe said. "Any questions?"

"Negative," Tony answered. "Over and out."

Frank moved out onto the highway. As he navigated through the traffic, Joe kept his eye out for the rest area where Hal and Tony were waiting. When it came into view, he picked up the mike again.

"Mr. P., we are passing your position now, over."

"Roger. Good luck."

Joe replaced the mike on its bracket. A short time later Frank saw his exit and turned off. There was very little traffic, he was happy to see. He didn't want anything to discourage the hijackers from their attempt.

Less than a mile after they'd left the highway, they heard the wail of a siren from behind them. A patrol car, lights flashing, appeared in their rearview mirror.

"Can't be for us," said Frank.

Joe craned around to look at the car as it rapidly overtook them.

"It's MacReedy!" he exclaimed.

The deputy drew up beside the Hardys, and he waved at them, signaling for them to pull over. Pressing down on the brakes, Frank eased the rental car over to the shoulder of the road and stopped.

"Where are the rest of his men?" Joe wondered aloud.

"He must've sent them ahead," Frank guessed. "Or, you know, we might be over the county line, out of his jurisdiction. Maybe he's called in the state police on this, and he's just coming to observe."

MacReedy pulled onto the shoulder behind them. Getting out of the patrol car, he strolled up to the Hardys. Frank rolled down his window.

"Hello there," said MacReedy. Casually he drew his service revolver from its holster and stuck its barrel under Frank's nose. He smiled thinly. "Looks like you two are in for a change of plan."

Chapter

17

MacReedy kept his gun trained on Frank's head. Easing open the rear door of the car, he slid inside.

"Just drive, son," said the deputy. "And if you think you can pull some kind of fancy maneuver with this car before I put a bullet in your head, why, you just try it."

Frank stared from the gun to MacReedy and back to the gun again. MacReedy was in it with Gerard! What had they gotten themselves into?

"Where are we going?" asked Joe.

"I'll give you directions," MacReedy replied gruffly. He rested the barrel of his gun on the seat back behind Frank. "You two aren't quite as smart as you think you are."

"Meaning what, exactly?" Frank said, although

he knew very well what the deputy meant. Still, maybe they could get him talking, buy some time.

"Calling me up like you did and telling me everything. No sir, you boys aren't that bright after all. Your old man is going to be disappointed in you."

"Dad said that you were a good cop when he knew you," Frank went on, not taking his eyes from the road. He tried not to think too much about the gun a few inches from his neck. "He'll be disappointed in you, too."

"Good cop?" MacReedy made a harsh, ugly laugh. "Yeah, I *was* a good cop. I had what it takes. Guts, brains, ambition—the works. I ought to have gone a lot further than I did, but your daddy saw to it that it wouldn't happen that way. I busted a couple of crooks, and he blew the whistle on me, told my boss I'd cooked up a little evidence to make certain the bust would stick."

"Did you?" Joe asked.

"Sure I did! Those creeps were guilty, but they might've gotten off if I hadn't done what I did. But your old man—oh, no, mustn't bend a rule, better to let a couple of crooks get away than tamper a little bit with the evidence. He ruined my career. I'm lucky I made it this far—a lousy chief deputy in a county department."

Deputy MacReedy was really warming to his story now. "Well, I got tired of getting by on a chief deputy's pay, figured I could get my hands on more. And I did, too. Then you came along and tried to mess me up,'' MacReedy sneered, ''just like your daddy did once before. Only now, it isn't going to work. It's payback time, boys. There's a driveway just up ahead on the right. Turn into it.''

Frank swung the car into the driveway and felt it bump along on the uneven surface. The drive didn't look as though it was used much. It was covered with potholes and wild grass, and it opened into a cracked and weedy parking lot. At one end Frank saw a restaurant with shuttered windows. Obviously, the place had been closed for a long time.

They weren't alone. Frank noted the Lombard truck over to one side, and another tractor, without any trailer, not far away. Pat and Matt stood under the watchful eyes of Turk and the other three members of the gang, all of whom were armed. With them was Lou Gerard.

Joe's stomach lurched as he realized that none of the toughs wore masks. He and Frank had seen all the faces before. He breathed deeply, knowing that it was vital for him and Frank to keep their heads and not panic.

Joe read aloud from a faded sign in old English lettering that rested on the peak of the restaurant roof. ''The Coach House. How's the food here, MacReedy? Did you and Gerard get together here for planning sessions over a steak and a baked potato?''

"Always got time for a gag, huh?" said the deputy, opening the car's rear door. "Well, the last joke today is going to be on you. Get out, slow, and join your friends over there."

Seeing the new arrivals, Gerard walked over to meet them. "We've got some plans to work out," he told MacReedy. "Leave these two with the others and let's talk. We don't have much time."

"Relax, Gerard," said the deputy. "This place has been closed for years. Nobody's going to stumble over us while we're here."

"Bruno! Turk!" called Gerard. The tall thug who seemed to run the gang's operations came over with his short, squat assistant. "Take these two over to the truck. And don't let 'em pull any stunts!"

Bruno nodded and gestured with his pistol for the Hardys to walk in front of him. Turk couldn't resist gloating a little.

"Well, if it ain't the two wise guys! What's the matter, huh? Nothing to say? Cat got your tongue?" He laughed at his own cleverness. No one else did.

Matt's face registered his shock at seeing Deputy MacReedy holding a gun on the Hardys.

"MacReedy— You mean *he's*—"

"Crooked as a corkscrew," Frank finished. "And we went and called him up and dumped everything we knew in his lap. Are we a couple of dynamite detectives, or what?"

"Don't be hard on yourselves," Pat said. "You couldn't have figured on the man being a criminal. Why did he do it, I wonder?"

"He says he got tired of living on a deputy's salary," said Joe. "My guess is he's getting a nice cut of this operation and that Gerard was planning on expanding the operation by squeezing every trucking company he could reach. Having a lawman on the payroll would be useful in a lot of ways. He could give you inside dope on what the police were doing. In a pinch he could tamper with evidence or deliberately screw up an arrest so a case would be dropped in court."

"Do you know any of these guys?" Frank asked Matt in a low voice, gesturing toward the hijackers. "We know who Turk is, but do these others all have trucking experience?"

Matt nodded. "That big guy, Bruno—he used to work for an outfit I worked for before I started Lombard. Everyone suspected he was padding his expenses and stealing stuff from his shipments, but nobody would face up to him—too big and too mean.

"One of the other two I've seen around, maybe at the truck stops getting a cup of coffee. But he's a trucker, I could tell from the way he moved my rig over here before. I figure they're all truck drivers who either couldn't get honest jobs or didn't want to."

They talked quietly until Lou Gerard came over and stood in front of them.

"Leonard Garry, I presume," said Frank. There wasn't any point in concealing what they knew, and he was curious about a few things.

The union man smiled. "You did some homework. You're smart, kid, but you'd have been smarter to stay out of the deep water, where the sharks are."

"Why'd you knock off your buddy Mickey Vane?" asked Frank. "That kind of has me puzzled."

Gerard sighed. "The man was stupid and had a bad case of big eyes. It's a dangerous combination. His orders were to warehouse the components we stole and maybe eventually sell them overseas—a long way from here, in any case.

"Instead, he set up that warehouse to sell off the goods here, only a few miles from where they'd been stolen. See what I mean—stupid and greedy! So we shut him down. Permanently. Just like we're going to do with you."

Joe didn't like the direction the conversation was taking. "And the check to Vane—forged, right?" he asked quickly.

Gerard grinned and nodded.

Bruno had unhitched the Lombard trailer from its tractor, Joe saw, and was now backing the other tractor into place. Deciding to take advantage of Gerard's talkative mood, he tried to buy some additional time.

"What now, Gerard? Or Garry, or whatever

your real name is? Are your bags packed for a quick getaway?''

Gerard looked sad for a moment. "I really thought I had a sweet setup here. Once Lombard went out of business, I figured every other trucking company in the area would line up to make their payoffs and avoid the same thing happening to them. It would've been nice—if you hadn't gotten in the way. But there are other cities, other false IDs, and lots of money floating around, if you know how to pick it up."

"What are you doing with the shipment on that truck?" Joe asked.

"I'm letting Bruno and his men have the contents of the truck," Gerard told him. "They deserve a little bonus, something more than we paid them. After all, now they have to start a new life somewhere else, and that can be expensive. So they can sell the electronics and split the take. Treat your help right, and they won't get mad at you. Isn't that right, Mr. Simone?"

Matt glared at him but refused to speak.

"Truck's just about ready to go, boss," called Bruno. "A couple of minutes more."

"Good," said Gerard. "The sooner we're out of here the better. MacReedy!"

The lanky deputy came over.

"We're just about set to go. You coming?"

"No," MacReedy said. "I think I'll stick around here. There won't be any witnesses to tie me to this whole thing, and I expect that I should do pretty well for myself from now on."

"Speaking of 'no witnesses,' MacReedy," Gerard reminded the deputy, "you have that one last chore to carry out, don't you?"

"You bet," the deputy replied. MacReedy replaced his service pistol in his holster, and reaching into a small traveling bag standing nearby, he pulled out a big Magnum revolver.

"This gun is cold," he said to Gerard. "There's no way to trace it back to me. I've been saving it for a special occasion, and this is it. Icing two nosy kids who happen to be Fenton Hardy's sons is my idea of a *real* special occasion. Turk!"

The burly gangster trotted over, gun in hand. "Turk asked if he could help out," explained MacReedy, "and I told him he could."

Frank knew it would be useless to make any kind of move. He watched helplessly as MacReedy cocked his big pistol with a loud threatening click and pointed it at Joe. Turk faced Frank with his gun. Frank could hear Pat Mulvaney begin to cry softly, although he didn't dare turn to look at her.

"So long, wise guy," said Turk. With that, he pointed the barrel of the automatic directly between Frank's eyes!

Chapter

18

FRANK COULDN'T HELP STARING into the barrel of the gun, and as he did he wondered if it would be the last thing he ever saw.

Suddenly the deafening blare of a trucker's horn filled the air, breaking the tense silence. MacReedy and Turk looked over their shoulders, and Frank followed their gaze. Coming straight for the group, with a throaty diesel roar, was the huge bulk of an eighteen-wheeler! Chrome glittered on the cab, and Hal Brady's angry face, bent forward over the wheel, could just be seen through the tinted windshield as the truck charged across the parking lot.

MacReedy dived to one side. Turk tried to aim at the onrushing monster, but he couldn't keep his arm steady. His shot went wild, and a split second later the front of the truck struck him, knocking him several feet through the air and throwing his gun in another direction. Turk lay still.

Knowing that Turk was out of action, Frank looked quickly around. He saw that Bruno was pointing his gun at Brady's truck, which had come to a halt.

"Get MacReedy!" Frank snapped to his brother.

"It'll be my pleasure," Joe muttered. Making a dive for MacReedy, he grabbed his gun arm before the deputy could swing around for a shot at him.

Hal shoved his cab door open, intent on getting in his licks. Bruno raised his automatic and leveled it at Brady.

"Brady! Watch out!" Frank yelled. Even as he spoke he charged forward, hitting Bruno with a cross-body block behind the knees. The shooter's knees buckled, and his arm jerked just as he squeezed the trigger. The shot starred the glass of the truck window, just above Brady's head as he climbed down.

As Bruno fell, he dropped the gun, but he was quick as a cat. Spinning around, he lashed out with a kick that landed in Frank's stomach, and jarred him backward. He turned back for his gun—only to have Hal Brady land on his back and flatten him to the ground.

"No, you don't, you ape!" Brady growled, wrenching Bruno's arm around behind him.

Tony Prito had been watching all of this from the cab. Grabbing a heavy wrench from the tool kit, he started down from the cab. When he was halfway down, Tony saw that one of the other gangsters had his gun trained on Frank. Before the goon could fire, Tony flung the wrench as hard as he could, shouting, "Frank! Behind you!"

The heavy wrench struck the hijacker in the side of the head with a clank, and he pitched forward. Tony dropped to the ground and scrambled for the guy's gun.

Frank flashed Tony a grin. "Good arm!" he called.

Meanwhile, Joe parried MacReedy's attempt at a kick to the midsection with his own knee. Grasping the deputy's gun hand with both of his own, Joe twisted it hard and jerked it backward at a painful angle.

MacReedy yelped and dropped the gun. He pivoted, then threw an awkward roundhouse punch with his left. Joe managed to duck under and step inside the swing, hitting the renegade lawman with a short right cross to the jaw. MacReedy reeled back, and Joe followed up with a left hook just under the rib cage and a looping right uppercut that connected with the deputy's chin.

MacReedy fell hard and lay still. Joe picked up MacReedy's Magnum, scooping up his service revolver as well. Breathing hard, he looked down at the unconscious deputy. "All right!" he said softly, smiling to himself.

Bruno had managed to buck Hal Brady off him, but as he got to his feet, Frank clasped his hands together and slammed them down as hard as he could on the back of the gangster's neck. As Bruno collapsed, Tony darted in and grabbed his gun.

The last of the hijackers, seeing his three partners down, became suddenly aware that he was outgunned and outnumbered. Hastily, he dropped his weapon and raised his hands.

"Where's Gerard?" growled Brady, looking around. "Where's the little weasel who tried to knock me off? I want a piece of him!"

"Everybody freeze!" Gerard shouted.

Joe looked up from the fallen MacReedy and saw that in the midst of all the action and confusion, Gerard had managed to slide over and pick up Turk's automatic. He now stood with his left arm wrapped around Pat Mulvaney's neck. With his right hand, he held the automatic to her head.

"I'm getting out of here, and this lady is going to drive me. Anyone tries to stop me and she's dead! Let's go, honey. Take it real easy, now."

Using Pat as a shield, Gerard pushed her over to the Lombard tractor, now "bobtailed"—without a trailer attached. He shoved her up into the cab and followed her.

"Don't try to follow us," he warned. "I'll shoot her if you do!"

Prodded by Gerard's gun, Pat started the tractor and steered it from the parking lot, heading for the road.

"Are we going to let that creep get away?" Hal Brady demanded angrily.

"We can't risk Pat's life!" Matt shouted, equally angry.

"He's bluffing," declared Frank. "He won't shoot her while she's driving. Joe, let's move it!"

He raced for their rental car.

Joe quickly handed MacReedy's guns to Matt. "Frank's right. He won't risk crashing that rig. Take the guns and keep these goons on ice. Use some of the rope the cargo is secured with to tie 'em up."

Frank was already in the driver's seat and gunning the engine when Joe jumped in beside him. The car sped off even before his door was fully closed.

The car had more speed and maneuverability than the tractor, and before long Frank spotted the tractor ahead of them. He quickly closed the distance between them.

"Pull up alongside and match their speed!" Joe shouted.

"You going to board it?" Frank asked, accelerating and moving next to the tractor.

"You bet," Joe replied. His eyes were fixed

on the wall of the cab beside him. Opening the car door, he reached out and took hold of one of the metal climbing rungs. Carefully he began to pull himself up until he was able to hook the bottom rung with his right foot.

Glancing up, he caught a glimpse of Pat's worried face as she stared at the road ahead. Joe pressed hard against the side of the cab, so Gerard wouldn't be able to get a shot at him. He groped for another handhold, toward the back, and a metal bar welded to the chassis provided it. Moving his left foot next to the right, he extended his right leg for a foothold behind the cab. The concrete was whizzing by below him, and seeing it, Joe tightened his grip.

Using the fifth wheel assembly and the hardware on the back of the tractor, Joe carefully worked his way across the back to the passenger side, fighting the bumping and swaying of the speeding tractor all the way. Then he started his climb toward the door.

Glancing up, he saw that Gerard had rolled down his window and had his gun outside. Joe ducked behind the rear of the tractor before Gerard could get a shot off.

Then, planting his foot in a step set into the cab body, Joe reached up for the narrow door that led to the sleeping compartment behind the seats, hoping that it was unlocked. It was, and he opened it. With one quick movement, he pulled himself up by the handle and lunged inside the cab.

Gerard twisted around and reached his gun over the seat back. When the pistol and hand appeared, Joe seized his wrist. Bending the gun away from Gerard, he yanked hard, pulling him close. Then Joe threw a straight right at Gerard's jaw. The punch traveled only a foot but packed enough power to stun Gerard, who sagged against the back of the seat.

Joe pulled the automatic from Gerard's unresisting hand.

"Pull over!" he yelled to Pat.

As she stopped the rig on the shoulder of the road, Pat scowled at Joe. "That was a dumb stunt to pull!" she exclaimed. "I was all set to jam on the brakes and slam his head into the windshield." Then she smiled. "But thanks, anyway."

"Don't mention it." Joe grinned back at her. "It's all just part of our regular service. No extra charge. Now let's see where we can find a phone and call some *real* cops to haul this bunch away."

"There's one thing I want to know," Pat said, with a thoughtful look. "How did Hal find us in that old restaurant parking lot? Didn't MacReedy grab you and Frank right after you got off the highway?"

"Yeah, he did."

"Well?" she demanded, looking impatient. When Joe still didn't answer, Pat said, "Are you going to talk, or just sit there with that self-satisfied smile on your face?"

"Okay, okay, don't get all feisty. MacReedy couldn't see under the dash on that car from the backseat. So I knocked the CB radio's mike loose with my knee and poked at it with my foot till I hit the transmitting button. Then I said the name of the restaurant and tried to signal Hal that MacReedy had us. I just had to hope Hal knew where the Coach House restaurant was."

"*And* that MacReedy wouldn't see your move with the CB *and* that Hal would hear what you were saying *and* that he'd figure out what had gone down." Frank had parked the car and climbed up on Pat's side of the cab in time to hear Joe's explanation. "Pretty thin stuff. I wouldn't pat myself on the back too hard."

"Hey!" exclaimed Joe. "The bottom line is, it worked, right?"

"Just barely," Frank replied. "We almost bought it today."

"Almost doesn't count," Joe said with a grin. "This isn't horseshoes. Help me haul Gerard out of here and get him into the back of the car, and then let's find that phone."

Leaving the truck where it was for the time being, the three took the rental car and drove ahead to a gas station to call the state police. By the time they got back to the parking lot of the Coach House, the first squad cars were rolling in. The troopers were busy taking statements from Matt, Tony, and Brady and replacing the ropes that had been used to tie up the thugs with handcuffs.

When the Hardys and Pat rolled into the lot, Tony and Matt left off talking to the officers and ran over to greet them.

"You all right?" Matt asked anxiously. "How did you do it?"

"Where's Gerard?" demanded Hal Brady, coming up to the car.

"Trussed up back there with Joe covering him," Frank answered, pointing to the backseat as he got out of the car. "Everything okay here?"

More troopers arrived on the scene, and two of them took charge of Lou Gerard. Two more were bandaging the groggy Turk, who had regained consciousness and seemed to have suffered nothing worse than severe bruises and scrapes.

Joe shook his head at Brady. "You sure took your time getting here. An old gearjammer like you, I figured you would burn rubber and be right on our tail when we pulled in here."

"Get off my case!" yelped Brady in mock rage. "I wasn't sure where the Coach House was, exactly. I had to try a few blind alleys before I lucked out. And *I* thought I did pretty well just to work out that message you gave me on the CB."

"You did just great," Matt assured the trucker.

"You can haul freight for me anytime. *Both* of you," he added, turning to include Pat. "You're both my top drivers—at least, until Mike is able to team a rig again."

"Fair enough," Brady replied. "I had you pegged all wrong, Matt, and I'm sorry about that."

"That's in the past, now," Matt assured him. Then he reached out and hugged Tony.

"Nephew," he said, "I owe you, too. You're responsible for bringing in Frank and Joe, and you pitched in and did your share when things got rough."

"Aw, hey, forget it," Tony said. He tried to appear casual, but he was clearly delighted by his uncle's compliments.

"Forget it? No way!" Matt hollered. "You have a reward coming, and I don't want to hear any arguments! Let's see, now—you couldn't by any chance use an Ultratech CD player, could you?"

Tony dropped his casual air, and his eyes opened wide. "Could I? That's—you're—"

"Cut it out," Matt said gruffly. "You earned it. I still have a business, thanks to you—and to these two here."

He turned to Frank and Joe. "What can I say? You saved my bacon, fellas. Anything I can do for you, you got it. All you have to do is ask. Go ahead, name it."

"Well—" Frank said after a moment. "We

figure getting involved in a case like this is enough reward. Putting guys like MacReedy and Gerard and the rest behind bars is enough satisfaction.''

"Joe, does that go for you, too?" asked Matt. "Or would you like to learn more about big rigs? We could teach you."

"Uh—I mean, trucks are really interesting and all, but to tell you the truth, I already know as much about trucks as I want to. And anyway," Joe went on, "like Frank says, we don't accept rewards.

"Besides," he added, smiling, "I figure a date with Teri is a nice bonus. So I guess we're all square."

"Well, there's one thing I want to do," Matt said, "and I'm not taking no for an answer."

"What's that?" Frank asked.

"You're coming to dinner one night next week. My wife makes the best chicken cacciatore in the state. That invitation goes for all of you," he added, looking at Pat, Tony, and Hal Brady.

Joe laughed. "You talked us into it," he said. "We'll be there."

"And bring your appetites," Matt went on. "We're celebrating the rescue of Lombard Hauling!"

The next day the Hardys were at the mall, splitting a pizza with Tony Prito.

"I hooked up that CD player last night," Tony

told them, putting down his half-eaten slice. "I'm telling you, it sounds unbelievable!"

"That's great, Tony," said Joe. Suddenly, Joe caught sight of someone over Tony's shoulder. He nudged his brother, who was sitting next to him.

"Look who's here," he said quietly.

Frank looked around. Jeff Lanier had just come into Mr. Pizza. With a quick wink at Tony, Frank called, "Hey, Jeff! Over here!"

Jeff saw them, gave a casual wave, and strolled over.

"What's happening?" he asked. "Tony, did you buy one of those CD players at that warehouse? Were those prices unreal, or what?"

"They were unreal, all right," Frank said.

"But I didn't buy one," Tony went on.

"No? How come?" Jeff asked, smiling. "Still too much money for you?"

"It wasn't that," Tony told him. "I just don't like dealing in stolen merchandise."

Jeff's mouth dropped open. "*Stolen*—what—hey, come on, you guys, cut it out. That's not funny."

"No joke," Joe said, giving Jeff a serious look. "That's why the prices were so low. Everything for sale there was hot. You bought stolen goods, Jeff."

Jeff licked his lips, looking suddenly very nervous. "Well, I didn't know—I mean—"

"Ignorance is no excuse, Jeff," Frank said.

"You could be in real trouble," Tony added, being careful not to smile.

Beads of sweat broke out on Jeff's forehead.

"You're seventeen, right, Jeff?" asked Joe.

Jeff nodded.

Frank let out a low whistle. "That means you can be tried as an adult."

Joe put on a solemn face. "Uh-oh. And you know, the stuff they make you wear in prison is *really* the pits. The worst."

Jeff's normally pale skin now looked gray. "I'll—I'll give it back. I didn't know! Honest!"

Tony couldn't hold it in any longer. He burst out laughing, and Frank and Joe joined in.

Jeff just stared at them for a minute. Then he got mad.

"Real funny, you guys!" he muttered, and stalked away.

"Hey, really, Jeff," Frank called out after him, "better turn that CD player in to the sheriff. It's evidence in a crime investigation."

Jeff stopped but didn't turn back. Then he walked out of Mr. Pizza.

When the laughter died down, Tony asked, "You think the police'll give it back to him?"

"No way," Joe answered. "If he'd thought about it at all, he'd have realized it was very suspicious."

Tony sat back. "So I wind up with a CD player, and he winds up with zip."

Frank picked up a piece of pizza. "It just goes

to show you, it always pays to be on the right side of the law.''

Joe nodded agreement. Then he said, ''But I have to say, that was a 'hot' sweater Jeff was wearing.''

The other customers in Mr. Pizza looked at them curiously as the three boys broke into loud laughter all over again.

Frank and Joe's next case:

A San Diego comic-book convention turns into a real blast when guest speaker Barry Johns, legendary publisher of Zenith Comics, is kidnapped. But the Hardys can hardly believe their eyes. Johns is abducted by two characters straight off the illustrated page—the Human Dreadnought and Flame Fiend!

Frank and Joe's investigation leads them into a confrontation with a rogues' gallery of comic-book villains come to life, each armed with sinister, super-sophisticated powers. But the boys are determined to have the last laugh by unmasking the criminal mastermind behind the crazy comic-book caper . . . in *The Last Laugh*, Case #42 in The Hardy Boys Casefiles™.